SURVIVING FAITHFUL

The Faithful Series Book 4

ANNA BISHOP BARKER

Home is where you crawl back to.

The brutal journey after you've earned the cruelest scars.

Where they wait

With blankets and drink and healing arms,

And no one turns you away.

— ANNA BISHOP BARKER

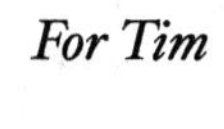

For Tim

PROLOGUE

Row Seventeen, Plot Forty-Two, Under The Big Oak Tree

He sat with his back propped up against the headstone. The sod under him was freshly laid and felt lumpy and hard under his ass. It was quiet, especially this early in the morning when the sun was barely a promise on the horizon. It had been pitch-black with no moon when he got there, and he had to use his big industrial flashlight. He had been there every night for the last two weeks, so he was vaguely surprised he still needed any light to find them.

Eighteen days.

They had been gone for eighteen days. *She* had been gone for eighteen days. The baby had been little more than a promise that had been broken.

A girl, they had told him. The ultrasound that would have given them the news had been scheduled for tomorrow morning.

No need for it now, of course.

Now Aponi and their baby girl lay under six feet and a few inches of frozen ground away from him.

He rested his head back against the cold, hard marble and closed his eyes. Did it make him a coward that he wanted to die too, but didn't have the guts to make it so? Survival was a concept he was intimately familiar with. Grief was not, and his mind was exhausted trying to reconcile the two. What had the preacher said?

"Someday you will understand God's plan, Kyle."

Why did they say shit like that? Because that is what it was—utter fucking, dog pile bullshit. If he lived to be 800, he would still not understand any of this fucked-up shit. He did not WANT to live long enough to understand it. Why didn't any of them get that and just leave him alone?

"There is no death, only a change of worlds."

Aponi had cross-stitched this Native American quote, framed the cloth, and hung it in their living room. He closed his eyes and pictured it hanging there, in the house he could barely tolerate going into now.

They all meant well. Were his heart still alive, he would have loved them for it. But the more his family and friends tried to do something, anything to help him, the less he felt capable of living. He wanted to lie down here, pull up the dirt over him, and sleep with them forever.

He wanted it, but he didn't do it, and with every day that passed he wondered why.

As Kyle Valentine sat on the cold dirt that covered the fresh grave of his wife and unborn daughter, he didn't see her sitting on the ground, just outside the iron fencing. He wouldn't have recognized her if he had seen her.

Olivia couldn't say exactly why she had followed him. She had heard the Harley pass her house every night for the past two weeks. It was hard to miss. There weren't many Harleys in Faithful. She knew it was Kyle, and she knew where he was going. Everyone in town knew where Kyle Valentine was spending his nights.

Something had made her walk to the cemetery tonight, and she hadn't brought Snape. The same force that had her follow the man, made her sit down to watch him. She knew she was invading a scene she should not be witnessing. But something kept her there. She sat on the concrete, shivering occasionally, until the big man finally got to his feet and walked the opposite way to where his motorcycle was parked.

Somewhere in the cosmos, something stirred in the stars.

Nineteen Rows Back and Fifty Feet to the East, Row Thirty-Six, Plot Two

Dr. Wilbur Hudson was buried next to his wife, Marlene. Olivia hadn't been there since she buried her father seven months earlier. But since she had been at the cemetery, it seemed wrong not to go visit, so when the Harley roared off, she had slipped in. Now she stood in the cold January air, gloved hands shoved into the deep, sheepskin-lined pockets of her coat. Her breath released in frosty puffs that drifted around her face.

Prior to her father's death, she hadn't visited her mother's grave on any regular basis since she left for college. There had been a time when she had ridden her bike there nearly every day. Marlene Hudson had died from the cancer in her breast, on a lovely spring day, when Olivia was eleven years old.

Eight months later, Olivia got her period. She had ridden to this very spot and stood on the grass that covered her mother's remains. She had screamed out her anger that Marlene Hudson had not been there to tell her what to do, what she needed. She had stood on this very spot and told her mother about the crush she had on Kyle Valentine in eighth grade. Sobs had rocked her teenage body when she asked her mother why Kyle didn't like her back. She had sat on this slight mound of earth and told her mother about the scholarships she had won, and the prom she hadn't been asked to, and the fight she had with her father when he had brought the woman home for dinner.

There had never been any answers. No words of wisdom, love, encouragement, or understanding.

Olivia remembered vividly standing beside Marlene Hudson's tombstone the day she was awarded the scholarship to UT. The silence was deafening. It always was. There were no words of pride, no doting smiles, no adoring arms. After that, she rarely visited. She thought about visiting, planned to visit. Something always came up. She never asked her father if he visited, and they had not once come together, not in all the years since.

Marlene Hudson's death defined Olivia's connection with her father. The life they led, the life her father had settled for, the foundation of the shaky relationship they had maintained, the bone-deep guilt she now felt, all of it had its roots here, in the cold Tennessee dirt. These two narrow plots of land had made Dr. Olivia Hudson who she was. For better or worse.

"I'm so sorry, Dad."

The tear was warm on her face for a moment.

"I'm so, so sorry."

The stirring in the stars intensified.

CHAPTER 1: HOME

Kyle

He came. Fucking finally. He had thought this would be a quick in and out, as it were. Wham, bam, one and done—twenty minutes, tops. He hadn't fucked a woman in three and a half years, for Christ's sake. When he jacked himself, it was over in less than ten minutes, especially if he had seen a picture or two of one of those English princesses.

As he pulled out and headed toward the hotel room john, he wondered idly why those two did it so easily for him. Especially the new one. Damn, she was hot. That Harry dude was a lucky guy. Kyle and Aponi had people who were their get out of jail free fucks, and his had always been Cher, circa 1979. That was, until he saw Meghan Markle and Cher was suddenly a distant second. It was the hair and the freckles. He was a sucker for freckles. He squeezed his eyes shut tightly.

He wasn't going there.

He dealt with the condom and washed his hands. Briefly, he looked at his face in the bathroom mirror. A lot had changed in three and a half years. His hair length, his fantasy fucks, his general outlook on this fucked-up world. He thought about the blonde back in the bed. Her name was Kaitlin Osborne. He met her at the gym. She was nice, had a great smile, and great tits.

This was their first and, he knew, only date. It was their first and only date, not because she was blonde or a bad lay. This was their only date because he was honest enough with himself to know he wasn't interested in another date or another fuck. It had nothing to do with her hair color or flawless skin or her inability to make him come in less than twenty minutes.

He wouldn't be seeing her again because there was no point in hurting what was most likely a decent woman. She hadn't led him to think she was looking for anything more, but it was not cool to take the chance when he knew there would never be anything more with her. There would never be anything more with her because Kyle was broken.

Broken in a way that he couldn't be fixed.

Suddenly, he felt so tired. Lowering his head until it hung down between his massive shoulders, his big hands braced on the sides of the sink.

"I'm tryin', babe. I really am. But, fuck, I miss you."

Three Weeks Later

"Go home."

Kyle moaned in his sleep, throwing out an arm, his hand connecting with the side of the cabin in the narrow space.

"Uyehi, go home."

The voice was clear, the tone vehement. Both were

so familiar that he jackknifed into a sitting position. Forgetting where he was, he neglected to make allowances for his size and promptly slammed his head into the low-hanging ceiling of the boat's sleeping berth.

"MOTHERFUCKIN' HELL!"

At the epithet and his sudden movement, the big gray cat that had been sleeping next to him dug his claws into Kyle's thigh, deep enough to draw blood, and sprinted out of the bed like the hounds of hell were upon them.

"GODDAMN IT TO FUCKING HELL!"

Kyle didn't know what hurt more—the contact between his considerably hard head and the teak bulkhead or the cat's talons sinking into skin that was not three inches away from his dick. He fell back into the pillows and rubbed first one and then, more gingerly, the other. Everything seemed to be in working order. He and Beast were going to have a conversation. The damn cat needed to sleep somewhere else, preferably not on Kyle's bed, or at the very least, not so close to his johnson.

Assured he wasn't going to lose consciousness or his balls, he remembered what had initiated the ruckus in the first place. The voice. No. Her voice. *Aponi's voice.* It had been as clear in his head as if she had been there in the bed beside him. Which she was not, could not be. But it had been her voice, nonetheless.

"Go home."

"Uyehi, go home."

"Husband, go home."

Carefully nursing his forehead and his crotch, he

rolled out of the too-short berth. The voice, *her voice*, still rang in his ears. He heard it. He fucking *heard* her as if she were in the room, alive, slightly annoyed, and impatient with him. She had been annoyed with him a lot, so he knew the tone well.

"Go home."

His trip into la-la land might finally be over. He was alone in a thirty-two-foot fishing boat, in the middle of the Gulf of Mexico, and he had just heard his dead wife tell him to go home. He didn't think she meant the marina in Clearwater, his home base, either. He knew what she meant. Hell, hadn't he been dancing around the thought himself for the last six months? Just last weekend, one of the charter members had asked him where he was from. He had nearly lied, made up some story to stop the questions from coming. Instead, he had spent twenty minutes talking about Tennessee, the hills, the music, the food. His guts and insides had ached when the conversation had ended. He pushed the memory aside as he entered the small toilet.

The head. He grinned wryly to himself. Sometimes the jokes wrote themselves. He finished in the small toilet and headed aft to the sitting area and galley, bracing his feet automatically to adjust his balance. Three years of living on a boat gave you sea legs, something he thought he would never get in his first months on the vessel. Now he felt physically off-balance on dry land. Apparently, he was becoming mentally off-balance, as well. He snorted to himself derisively. Sam would have a field day with this if he ever learned of it, which was not going to happen. His best friend did not need any ammo to give him shit with, and Sam Beckett never missed an opening.

Damn, he missed the guy. They spoke occasionally, texted often, but it wasn't the same as sitting on a porch and shooting the shit. He hadn't gone back for the wedding when Sam married Delilah. She had called him, told him it was okay, she understood, that Sam understood. He should have gone. He had missed his best friend's marriage ceremony because he didn't want to deal with the looks and the questions and the words of love and support.

Christ, he was an ass and a coward.

It would serve him right if Aponi started to haunt him. He knew she would put an ectoplasmic foot up his ass for behaving as he had for the last three years. He deserved it. He had left people who cared about him, cut himself off, and left them to deal with his residual shit. Meantime, he ran off and became a fishing boat captain with a psychotic cat.

"You need to get your shit together, Kyle. Then you need to get your country ass back to Tennessee. You've got another six months. Then I'm coming down there myself and dragging you back to Faithful by your testicles." His aunt, Rhonda, didn't mince words. This had been her voicemail, left on his phone three weeks ago, when he refused to pick up when she called.

He knew it was no idle threat.

Stepping up to the helm, he ducked his head under the Bimini and prepared to fire up the engines. The sun was just peeking up over the horizon. The Gulf waters were quiet, nearly smooth as glass. Kyle sat back in the captain's chair for a moment, breathing in the early November air. He closed his eyes. It was the most peaceful place on earth, out there in a realm that was not ruled by humans. It was exactly what he had needed when they were taken from him. The problem was, it had become more of a place to hide than a place to actually live.

"Uyehi, go home."

Slowly, he opened his eyes. The phantom pain in his gut was back. The acute ache of grief that had hounded him for months and months had faded. It still could come in a wave and leave him weak, but it didn't happen often, and he had learned long ago how to keep his feet when it hit. The ache had been replaced by a bone-deep gnawing pain he had been reluctant to put a name to. He was such a coward; he couldn't even admit he was homesick.

And lonely.

He was so fucking lonely that some nights he couldn't breathe, it was so overwhelming.

Olivia

"Miss Pauline, you have got to stop giving him table scraps, especially chicken bones. Cooked bones splinter in the stomach."

Olivia shut the mesh door to the small crate that was bolted to the walls and stacked on top of similar, larger crates in the hospital area of the clinic. The tiny, white Maltese mix she had slid into the crate curled into a ball and promptly fell asleep, the trauma of the last couple of hours taking their toll. Olivia turned from the wall of cages to the tall, thin woman with iron gray hair, who stood next to the crates, a wad of tissues pressed to her face.

Pauline Jenkins was an unmarried, sixty-three-year-old woman with no children. A pharmacist by trade, she had once owned a small drugstore in town that had been bought out by a chain some years back. She had also once had a housemate, a woman of similar age named Marion, but Marion had died quietly one day ten years or more ago, and Miss Pauline had been alone since. It wasn't really talked about, but it was common knowledge, Miss Pauline wasn't interested in men. Faithful was a loving town, full of mostly good people, but it was not immune to ignorance, prejudice, and hate. No one had brought Miss Pauline a casserole or offered to mow her lawn when Marion had passed. There had been no flowers sent, no cards of sympathy.

Olivia reached out a hand and took the older woman's free one. Olivia hadn't made a casserole either. She felt a profound sense of shame for that as she took the woman's trembling fingers in hers.

"He's going to be fine. I mean, Grover is fourteen years old, but he's too ornery to die from a chicken bone." She forced a grin because she knew Miss Pauline liked a good joke any day of the week. It worked. The woman's lined face lost some of its fear and a slight smile curved her thin lips. Olivia squeezed her fingers and released her grip, curving an arm around the woman's shoulders and guiding her toward the door that led out into the hallway. "I'm going to watch him until tomorrow around lunch time, then you can come take him home."

They moved down the hall, Olivia guiding the way with her arm still around the woman. "And don't worry about the stay. I'm not going to charge you for the hospital, since I'm mostly keeping him so I can play with him in the morning." She couldn't go back and mow the woman's lawn or offer her condolences and comfort, but it was never too late to change your own heart and give of yourself to someone else.

Abruptly, the older woman stopped walking, turned, and pulled Olivia to her in a bone-crushing hug, a hiccupping sob escaping her. Olivia immediately returned the embrace. She felt the woman's body shaking against hers and tightened her arms. She knew all too well how much an animal could help fill the crater loneliness carved into your soul. Grover was an elder dog. She was going to talk to Miss Pauline about getting him a younger friend when things settled down. The little white dog was a scrapper, but he wasn't immortal.

Shakily, Miss Pauline let Olivia go. Her voice was low but strong. "I'll pay, Olivia." No one over the age of fifty called her Dr. Hudson. That was her father. Olivia risked offending the woman by moving her hands to grip the woman's upper arms, and her eyes held Pauline Jenkin's watery but stubborn stare.

"No, you won't. Don't hurt my feelings by turning me down." Olivia felt slightly uncomfortable for using what amounted to emotional blackmail, but no way was she taking a payment for this night from this woman. The two women had a stare down for long moments, then Pauline stepped back and straightened her shoulders. Sniffing loudly, she muttered, "Your father always said you was as stubborn as a mule. I'll expect you to accept a pie when I pick him up tomorrow, you hear me?" She stepped away from Olivia and the air lightened. "What do you like, apple or pecan?"

Olivia turned with the woman and they moved toward the double wooden doors that led out of the office and into Olivia's graveled driveway and small parking lot. She pulled the heavy door open and they continued walking toward the black SUV that was parked haphazardly across the drive. Two hours ago, Pauline Jenkins did not care about parking spots.

"Pecan. And why don't you make it later this week? I can have it fresh with my Sunday dinner." Olivia did not want the woman to go home and make a complicated recipe after the afternoon she had experienced. They reached the woman's vehicle and she turned to face Olivia. The knowing expression on her face said she was aware of what Olivia was doing, but she wasn't going to mention it just then.

"All right, I'll bring it over on Saturday." She stepped up into the SUV, settled herself, and had her hand on the ignition when she turned her eyes back to Olivia's. "Thank you, Olivia. Your father would be proud." The woman's voice lowered, and she looked away from Olivia. "Give Grover a kiss for me, will you?"

Olivia stepped back, giving the woman the space she sensed she needed. "I will, Miss Pauline. Drive careful. I'll see tomorrow around one."

The woman nodded, then took a deep breath, her hands gripping the wheel as she appeared to rally her strength, and, without further comment, she backed out of the driveway. Olivia watched her go, replaying the words "Your father would be proud" in her head. He would be. She didn't deserve it, but he would be.

She had turned toward the clinic entrance, her mind beginning the mental checklist of all she had to get done before closing, when she heard the Harley. She froze with her hand on the wood panel of the door. The last time she heard that sound had been over three years ago. She grimaced. That was absurd. Motorcycles had driven down her street innumerable times in the last three years. Today was no different.

"He's home."

Unbidden, and strangely, not in her own internal voice, the words registered into her consciousness.

Olivia pushed through the door and went back into her clinic, shaking off the breathless, weird feeling.

She missed the big, black Harley. She failed to see the huge, muscled man wearing aviator sunglasses, ancient jeans, and an equally ancient Led Zeppelin tee shirt. She didn't see that he wore no helmet.

She also missed the small, orange-furred, lifeless body that had lain on the corner edge of her front lawn since just before dawn that morning.

CHAPTER 2: THE COOKOUT

Olivia

Why did freckles make you look about twelve years old, when you were nearly thirty-six? Olivia sighed and threw the foundation brush in the general direction of her makeup tray. The choices were, look like a Vegas show-girl with pancake makeup that was an inch thick, or like she belonged back in junior high with braces and an NSYNC backpack. She had never wanted to change her dark red hair, but she would have paid a high price to have her freckles zapped into kingdom come.

Sighing again, she adjusted the long braid that hung over one shoulder and twirled the wavy tendrils that escaped near her cheek. Regarding her reflection, she saw what she always saw: a face that was a bit too round, lips that were a bit too full, eyes that just missed being an interesting shade of blue-green, lashes that were long but reddish-blonde and needed Herculean amounts of mascara to be seen. She pulled distractedly on the fili-greed silver earring that dangled amongst what she hoped was the artfully escaping hair at her neck. Those damned freckles. She could look sophisticated were it not for those annoying little brown flecks.

Blowing out a snort of disgust, she turned away from her reflection and left the bathroom. Olivia was many things but sophisticated was not one of them. If she was honest, she didn't really want to be sophisticated, but it would have been nice to be at least interesting. The best she could do was cute on a good day, and today she wanted to look fascinating. Yes, today of all days, and for the first time in a long time, she wanted to look something more than the cute girl with the freckles and the smile.

She could tell her ego lies, but self-delusion was something she tried to steer clear of. She knew exactly why she was fussing in front of a mirror, something she rarely did. Her motivation for selecting the wraparound top, that discreetly accentuated her breasts, was a deliberate choice. She knew everyone who was going to be at this cookout. They were her friends, her furry patients' owners, some relatives. Everyone attending would be of at least nodding and waving acquaintance. If there were a stranger at this gathering, it would be because someone she knew had brought them as a guest. She was unconcerned about any of that, and she wasn't mentally bitching about freckles because of it. She certainly wasn't wearing her best bra because of it.

Olivia was low-key fretting about her appearance because *he* was going to be there. Thirty minutes from right then, she and Kyle Valentine were going to be in the same place. She would have to talk to him, at the very least, say hello. She hadn't seen him in over three years, since that night at the cemetery. She hadn't spoken directly *to* him since she was fifteen.

That conversation, carried out in the high school parking lot after a football game, still made her cringe, all these years later. God, why did the wounds you received as a teenager never really heal?

"Sorry, kid. I don't date children. Especially scrawny little redheaded ones with no tits."

She closed her eyes. She could still hear his voice inflection, the mixture of scorn and immature, jackass man cruelty. It had taken her weeks to get up the courage, but she was a modern young woman, she told herself, and she could ask a guy out. She had sat in the bleachers with her best friend, Jeanine, and surreptitiously watched Kyle and Sam Beckett drink beer under the bleachers while the game played out. Then she followed him, this wild, dangerous guy, with the long hair and the tattoos on his forearms; this big, beautiful boy-man who she had worshipped from afar for an entire year. She had caught up to him at the door of his rusted, banger, puke-green Ford pickup truck. She had taken her heart and her fifteen-year-old allotment of courage into her hands and asked him if he would like to go for pizza.

He had looked her up and down, snorted with laughter, and shattered her heart.

"Sorry, kid. I don't date children. Especially scrawny little redheaded ones with no tits."

Olivia had mooned about Kyle Valentine through most of eighth grade and all of ninth. She knew his reputation was bad, and she also knew her father would never have allowed her to go out with him. She had approached him anyway, and the situation had taken care of itself. All her ridiculous fantasies of him looking into her eyes and leaving behind his untamed, scandalous, bad boy ways had gone down the proverbial toilet. She had gone home, burning with humiliation, and cried herself to sleep. She had hated him for a while. She had plotted revenge. Then the pendulum of adolescent emotion had swung, as it was want to do, and her crush faded.

Late in her junior year, she had steadily dated a boy from church. Matt Lord had been nice, kind, and devoted. They had parted ways right before graduation and he had moved with his family out west somewhere.

She had gone to college and lost her virginity to a nice guy from her chemistry lab. She had been briefly engaged in her last year of vet school, but it hadn't worked out, mostly because he cheated on her with a research assistant. She had come home to Faithful, took over the veterinary practice from her father, dated occasionally, but nothing serious.

When tragedy took Kyle Valentine's wife and unborn child, she had followed him to the cemetery for reasons she still could not understand. She hadn't pined in a state of unrequited love for him. In truth, once she went to college, he barely crossed her mind. The night at the cemetery she finally put down to a reaction to his grief and her own unresolved mourning for her father.

Olivia had a reputation as a "nice girl" and that was fine with her. She had built a life in her hometown that was satisfying, if not terribly exciting. She was friendly, outgoing, and didn't take life or herself too seriously. Whenever she was getting her hair done or a manicure, someone would try to fix her up with a cousin/brother/friend. She usually went on the dates, and the regret ratio was about 2:1 in favor of regret. Laura Beckett had fixed her up more times than she cared to count, until she finally begged her friend to stop. She felt herself settling into the status of the practical, asexual town vet, who didn't want to settle down with a man and children. Hell, she had even gone on a date with the resident handsome-as-a-movie-star John Valentine. They had ended up laughing about overpriced steak and bad beer, and now he was marrying his housekeeper.

Faithful wasn't the big city and it was in the Appalachian Mountains. She might be perceived as the practical spinster in a town that hadn't caught up to the New York speed of life, but, like most stereotypes, this one held little reality. Few people had ever seen her movie collection. If they had, most would be shocked. The "nice girl" with the red hair, sensible jeans, and ready smile was heavily into intense. *Blue Valentine*, *Punch Drunk Love*, *The English Patient*, *The Bridges of Madison County* were just some of the movies in a collection that was overwhelmingly romantic, intense, and full of tearjerkers. Dr. Olivia Hudson liked her love stories deep and passionate.

She wanted a love that was deep and passionate, longed for it, in fact. The only thing she wanted more than to be able to set things right with her father was to find a man who would love her like Nicholas Cage loved Meg Ryan in *City of Angels*. Any guy who would give up being an angel for you had the right idea about love. But there were no men like that in east Tennessee, at least none for her.

Sitting down on her bed, she pulled on the buttery-soft, leather knee-high boots she had splurged on when she last went shopping in Knoxville. It was November, it was cool, and the cookout was in the backyard of Jake and Laura Prescott's farmhouse. The jeans, the blouse, and the boots would be appropriate. If her cleavage made a discreet appearance when she shook Kyle Valentine's hand, well she wasn't going to stop herself from getting a little revenge for his comment when they had been teenagers.

But this was it. This was her measure of pettiness for the year, and no one would know but her. She mentally shook off any deeper feelings, grinned to herself, and picked up her purse.

She suddenly remembered the sound of the motorcycle the other night, the breathless feeling of a voice in her head that wasn't her own.

"He's home."

Kyle

The sound system was pounding out Brooks and Dunn's "Boot Scootin' Boogie," and he was on his second Sam Adams Boston Lager when he saw her. She was standing next to the line of long picnic tables that held the food, holding a bowl of something and talking to Laura Beckett. She was turned away from him, bending to set the bowl in the space on the table, and he would have had to be blind not to notice her ass—generous, shapely, and presented to perfection by the jeans she wore. He was unaware of how long he had been admiring her ass when he was jolted out of his regard by a sharp poke to his rib cage.

"Man, put your tongue back in your mouth."

Kyle jerked his head around at the poke and the comment. Sam Beckett and Kyle's cousin, John, had joined him where he stood, under the awning of the bricked patio area that skirted the expansive lawn of the farmhouse. They each held their own beers, obtained from one of the large metal buckets filled with ice and drinks that dotted the patio. It was Sam who had delivered the elbow to his ribs and the admonition.

"Hey, fucker, I was just admiring the scenery. What, is she someone's wife?" He hoped not. He really wanted to keep admiring that ass.

They all three regarded the hot as hell—to his way of thinking—redhead, and he was surprised when it was John who spoke. His second closest friend and cousin was usually quiet in nature and didn't wade into their more boisterous bullshitting. This was shaping up to be the first semi-normal conversation he'd had with his friends since getting back a week ago. Tomorrow was going to suck, and he wanted to enjoy today. He wanted to fall back into the superficial, lighthearted bullshit of their younger days.

"That's Olivia Hudson, Doc Hudson's daughter. She came back to town to run the vet clinic a few years back." Sam took a drink from his bottle and continued, "She's become friends with Delilah and Laura, since she takes care of all the dogs."

Kyle had a vague memory of a tall, gangly girl with

red hair and freckles he would see around town and maybe at school. He thought they might have spoken once, but the memory was cloudy, as were a lot of things from his younger days. He had been too busy being a teenaged fuck-up back then to really pin down a lot.

Kyle took a hit of his beer, the icy liquid smooth and easy going down. There was no way she had looked like that in high school. He would have hit it hard if she had. He hit everything he could reach hard back then.

"She's a nice woman. Took her out to dinner once and she was great." John's voice held nothing but respect. Kyle was a tad shocked. John was ass over tea kettle in love with the woman he was set to marry after Christmas, so it was surprising the guy even remembered another woman's name.

"She still single?" Now, why did he ask that? He was not back here to start building a social life just yet.

He felt surprise and awkwardness in the ensuing silence. Back in the day, these men would have been all over giving him shit if he expressed interest in a woman. Fuck. He didn't want his friends to feel uncomfortable around him. This wasn't the first prolonged silence of the day. It had happened with nearly everyone in town, and it was his own damn fault. If he had come home sooner, worked on his shit with the people around him who could have eased the pain, maybe, he wouldn't be standing here in an uneasy silence with the two people who knew him best in the world.

Fuck, he was such a selfish piece of shit sometimes.

"She's single. Far as I know, anyhow."

That was Sam. John held his silence and looked down

at the bottle in his hand, suddenly fascinated with the label. Kyle knew what that meant. John had something to say, and he was taking his usual measured time before he let loose. He had a feeling he might not like what the other man was about to say.

He was right.

John raised his head and looked Kyle in the eye. His regard was caring, but there was also caution and a vague warning in his voice when he finally spoke.

"She's a good, decent woman. Not someone for a hit and run." His eyes held Kyle's without wavering, and Kyle felt a stab of anger run through him.

"What the fuck is that supposed to mean, man? I just asked if she was single. I'm not planning to take her to the Motel 6 tonight." He felt way more pissed than the situation warranted. He was thirty-nine, not nineteen. His horndog ways had been many and varied, but they had also been over the minute he hooked up with Aponi. But this was John, and John was family. He wasn't being a dick. At least he wasn't trying to be, Kyle hoped.

Kyle took a deep breath and got his temper back on the leash before he continued. This needed to get laid out. His friends and family needed to know from jump where his head was at.

He turned slightly so he was facing both Sam and John. He took another breath, took another slug of beer, and said what needed to be said.

"Look, okay, I might have deserved that once. But give me a little credit here, man. I'm not headed back to high school shit." He slugged back the remainder of his beer, turned slightly at the waist, and threw the bottle into the bin closest to him provided for empties. His voice was aggressive when he continued.

"I'm home. I plan on staying for a while. I'm putting the house on the market tomorrow, renting a place out on 321. I'm gonna take back over running the studio, at least part time, if that's all right with you and Jake." He directed this last at John.

"I sold my boat. I'm going to start looking around for a full-time job next week." He paused, but neither man spoke. When he resumed, he modulated his tone and deliberately let go of the residual anger he felt after John's admonition.

"I just want to breathe and work on getting some peace, all right? Fuck, you guys are my best friends, and I did everything but cut you off for the last three years, and I feel like dogshit about it, okay? So can we all just tongue kiss, sing "I Will Always Love You," and admire the lovely Doc Hudson's ass for a hot Nashville minute?"

"Dolly's version or Whitney's?" The voice came from right behind him. It was slightly husky, had a faint East Tennessee twang, and the edge of smart-ass was evident. Kyle glanced at the men in front of him and felt his stomach twitch with an exceedingly unfamiliar feeling. It was a combination of discomfort and embarrassment. John's lips were twitching, and Sam had a shit-eating grin the size of Texas spread across his face.

"She's right behind me, isn't she?" He directed the question at them both. John quirked an eyebrow and Sam's grin widened. The voice at his back was rich with humor when it replied, "Yes, she is."

Well, fuck him.

Charlie

Rocking them once they fell asleep was something that had to be done, even if they had been asleep a long time before they got found. And it was done. Then this poor little thing was going on its last trip.

She was going to pay for what she had done. Oh, yes, oh, yes, oh yes. She was going to pay. But first she was going to take care of the poor little things.

Rock-a-bye, baby, in the treetops. Rock and rock and rock.

CHAPTER 3: TABLE

Olivia

He really was cute.

Olivia supposed it was odd to call a man of his size and bulk cute, but his evident embarrassment when he turned around to look at her had been ridiculously cute. The uncomfortable bra and time spent on her makeup had been worth the price of admission, just to see that look on his face. It didn't entirely compensate for her teenage humiliation, but it was close. The debt for her rejection at fifteen had been paid when she realized that he well and truly didn't remember inflicting it.

John had introduced them. Otherwise they might still be standing in Jake and Laura Beckett's backyard staring at each other; her with glee and Kyle with mortification. Olivia would bet a lot that Kyle Valentine didn't get his trunks in a truss often, and it was delicious to see him mentally squirm just a little.

Yes, definitely cute.

"Kyle, this is Olivia Hudson." John had paused, smiled his movie star smile at her warmly, and elaborated. "Dr. Olivia Hudson. Olivia, I don't know if you remember Kyle Valentine, my cousin, and today's jackass of the day."

She held out her hand. He took it in his dinner plate-sized paw. "Liv, nice to meet ya. You can call me Mr. Jackass." He grinned at her, the change in his eyes and demeanor making her stomach do a slight flip. The smart-ass, horndog heartbreaker was still inside, even if it had been toned down by maturity and life experience. The evidence was a grin made of pure devilish mischief and a spark in his eyes.

She grinned back and relished the warmth of his hand. His fingers were slightly rough, his grip firm. "Mr. Ass, it's nice to meet you. My name is Olivia. And we have met before, although it's been years." She slid her hand from his, but the heat of the contact made her palm tingle. She saw uncertainty cross his face for a nanosecond and wondered how often that happened, too. She would bet not very. In fact, she thought she might have imagined it as a cocky smirk took its place.

"Have we now?" His deep voice took on a flirtatious tone that sounded practiced, but not altogether sincere. "How could I possibly have forgotten meeting you?"

Sam made a snickering sound. "That's my cue to go get another beer." The tall, blond man turned, slapping Kyle on the shoulder. "Good luck, my man. See ya later, Olivia. Come on, John. I'm fairly certain Mr. Jackass can take care of himself."

She watched as John Valentine stood still and simply looked at Kyle for several long seconds, seeming to communicate without words. Neither man spoke. Then he turned his regard to Olivia. "You let me know if I need to kick his ass in any way, would you?"

Unsure of what had just passed between the two, she softened her grin and smiled. "Oh, I'm sure he's basically harmless. And he does admire my ass, so there's that." She turned her eyes back to Kyle and the smile on her lips became wicked. "Besides, I'm going to enjoy telling him the story of how he broke my heart and sent me to the convent when I was a mere girl."

The two other men moved away. She was only peripherally aware of them because she now had his full attention. Having the power of the man fully concentrated on her was a bit much. He was so tall, nearly a head taller than her, and she was five feet nine in her sock feet. He was also big, his shoulders massive and muscled. The magnitude of the man was barely contained by the navy tee shirt he wore that had, incongruously, a picture of Stevie Nicks emblazoned across the front in all her witchy-woman glory. His hair was dark brown, cut close on the sides, but with a somehow boyish mop of curls on top. The skeleton tattoo she remembered was still evident on his thick, veined forearm, but now it had been joined by others peeking out from under the tight sleeves of his tee shirt.

He had the scruff of maybe a two-day-old beard, and intense whiskey-brown eyes that somehow reminded her of Snape when he was begging for a treat. No, that wasn't exactly right. As she continued to stand in front of him and stare into his face, she saw it. Those eyes might have once been filled with nothing more than teenage delinquent bravado, but that was no longer the case. There were shadows and demons there now. Now they were a lot more interesting if a bit uncomfortable to investigate. She was aware of what had caused some of those shadows.

She came out of her thoughts when his deep voice sounded. "So we met when you were a wee child, huh? What, did I order a root beer float from you at the Krispy Kone?" The tone was only slightly mocking, but teasing. It still stung just a whisper, enough for her to retort without gauging her words.

"No. You told me I was scrawny and had no...uh... chest." Her voice faltered over the actual term he had used.

She watched as his dark brows knitted in a frown, and he didn't respond immediately. When he did respond, it was not what she had anticipated. She hadn't planned on having this conversation, so she had put zero thought into what he would say if she ever confronted him about their meeting, so many years ago. Back in the day, she had imagined herself spouting off some brilliantly cutting speech, turning on some killer fuck-me heels, and sashaying away from his gaping shock. Once time and maturity took over and his rejection faded, her plans of revenge had faded as well. His reply and the faint hint of remorse in his expression made her regret bringing it up. She did not want to be the reason he felt anything negative.

"Jesus, I was an asshole."

There was no trace of humor in his voice or on his face. His warm brown eyes held no mocking, and the seriousness in them was surprising. They were talking about a childish conversation that was over twenty years old, after all.

"I did a lot of shit that I'm sorry for back then. I honestly don't remember saying that to you, but knowing my propensity for dickheadedness, I'm not surprised." He curved his lips, but it wasn't really a smile. His voice was. "Will it help if I tell you that being scrawny, and the alleged lack of a chest are not problems for you now?" Intuition told her this flirtatious comment was not meant to be provocative. It was a fallback way of communicating that felt safe to him. She unconsciously started to raise a hand. She nearly touched him. She wanted to tell him it was she who was sorry for bringing something up that was better left alone.

She had opened her mouth, but the words never formed. Laura Beckett and a couple of other people had come up to them, conversation had switched, and by the time there was another opportunity for her to talk to Kyle, he was gone.

She went home soon after, removed her boots and the medieval torture device of a bra, and took a shower. She fed Snape and checked on her part-time night tech, who stayed over in the basement bedroom attached to the clinic when there were animals in the hospital that required more intensive care. Assured that all was well, she came back up to the main living quarters of the rambling Southern house that had been in her father's family for generations, set the alarm, and went to bed.

She lay in her big bed with the white rail headboard. She thought about Kyle Valentine and his eyes with the sparks and the sadness, and she wondered what they looked like when he was happy. She remembered the vigil outside the cemetery fence she shared with him when his wife died. She considered all the times he had crossed her mind over the years since Aponi's death. She wondered why he had wisped through her memories so often after it happened, when before she had rarely thought of him since her adolescent crush faded.

People in town talked about him, of course, especially after he left. She had clients who brought him up occasionally, especially since he was quasi-related to half the town, and Faithful loved a good gossip. Kyle Valentine was one of the more interesting town citizens. He had made something of himself after the way he had come up, and to the folks in town that was something to be remarked over and commented on.

He had the martial arts studio. He taught the young wives how to defend themselves and the young kids how to deal with bullies. He had served his country. He had a job that served his people. He had that hair and those tattoos... and that bike. He played his music loud, he laughed loud; he lived loud.

And he had loved loud. When he and Aponi learned they were going to have a baby, he had stopped people on the streets to tell them the good news. Olivia had heard about it at the grocery store because Kyle had told everyone in line at the deli case, and she had overheard two aisles away. It was hard to miss that big, irreverent, booming voice.

She had also become good friends with Jake and Laura Beckett. Kyle had been Jake Beckett's nurse in his general practice, and Laura had been the target when

Aponi was killed in their office late one night. Over the last several years, Laura had talked to Olivia at length about her feelings of grief and guilt, so she knew exactly how Kyle had lost his wife and how he had dealt with the immediate aftermath. He had packed up three weeks after he lost her and moved to Florida, bought a fishing boat, and only called home for Christmas.

Now he was home. The question was, why was he home? Why were ideas of him suddenly filling her every random thought?

"He's home."

Why did a voice inside her head feel like it belonged to someone else?

Charlie

The poor little thing was still where it was left. That would not do. No. No. No. She had to find it and take care of it, the bitch. It was all a lie. She didn't care about the poor little things. No, no, no, she didn't. Now Charlie would have to go move the poor little thing, and sacrifice another. Charlie cared about all the poor little things, even the ones who had to be sent to God before they were ready.

Rock-a-bye, rock-a-bye.

Kyle

The house didn't look any different from the drive. The grass was cut, the bushes were trimmed, the walkway edged. The blinds were drawn, which wouldn't have been the case when he and Aponi lived there, but otherwise it looked the same as the day he left it three weeks after she died.

His wife had been shot in the back by a psycho, who

had come to her job looking for someone else. The bullet had severed her aorta and she had bled out on the floor of the medical clinic where she was working late. She bled out in the arms of his boss's then-girlfriend. He didn't get to say goodbye.

He didn't rail against the unfairness of it anymore. What was the point? It changed nothing and it answered no questions. The fact was it was one of those random horrors of life on earth that happened countless times to countless people. Aponi would have said it was part of the sacred circle, the balance of things. His wife had tried to teach him the philosophy of her Cherokee heritage, and in most aspects, he got it. The parts he didn't get, he respected as a part of her and of a people who were probably thousands of years older than he. He did not get how her bleeding all over a white tile floor, his daughter bleeding right along with her, brought any kind of fucking balance to anything.

Kyle had spent two tours in Afghanistan as a field medic. He knew there were a lot worse things that could happen to a human being. His wife had simply been in the wrong place at the way wrong time, and she had died. His unborn child had died. He had been angry. No, he had been raving-ass mad-as-a-shithouse rat for a while, and a bit too close to suicidal for a hot minute, or five. His grief had surrounded him, nearly suffocating him, for what seemed would be an eternity. It still could appear out of nowhere and take his breath away.

But like the survivor he was, he had fought back. The cliché of time had done its work, and he knew it had the day he woke up on the boat and realized his gut had gone from being filled with rage and grief to being just empty. That was when the isolation moved in. Oh, it didn't arrive with a moving van. It brought a suitcase a day until it had taken over every inch of his available soul. At first the boat was soothing, peaceful. But after nine months or so, the silence became too loud. Then he got Beast.

The emaciated, gray Russian blue showed up at his boat one morning and never left. He came with enough neediness to keep Kyle occupied for nearly a year, because it had taken that long to put some weight on the thing. Every morning Kyle had expected the cat to be long gone. But, although Beast blossomed into an enormous ball of gray fur and attitude, he never left. But you couldn't cook dinner with a cat. You couldn't watch movies with a cat. Well, you could try, but the finer points of *John Wick* were lost on the now sixteen-pound ball of fur and claws. Not to mention you couldn't make out with a cat.

So, Kyle eventually dated a bit. He slept with the blonde from the gym. After a few months he slept with a woman he met on a charter trip. He didn't return to the serial fucking of his youth, but it was enough.

That was a lie, of course. It wasn't enough. Not anymore. He had had sex, and he had made love, and he much preferred the latter.

Now, here he stood, at the front door of the house that had witnessed so much love and laughter. This house, along with the woman who had lived there with him, had changed him. They had shown him he was worthy of them. He had learned he always had been worthy of them, regardless of what his childhood might have said. His idea of balance had once been that he would spend his life, break his back, to deserve what he had been given. Instead he was here to go through the house one last time before it was sold, and that part of his life was over and done.

He turned the key and stepped over the threshold into the room that had been the living room. The house wasn't big. It had two bedrooms and a bath and a half, no dining room, and no basement. The kitchen was a galley, and the porch was narrow. The backyard had a fence and a small concrete patio. It was no different than thousands of other lower middle-class houses in thousands of other small Southern towns.

This diminutive brick house on this narrow street had been the first dwelling he could ever truly call his home. Rhonda had done her best, given him a bed in her basement, fed him, clothed him, sent him to school, loved him in her way. But Kyle was always keenly aware he had no idea where, or even who, his father was, and his mother had left him to go live her life elsewhere. He was a guest, a burden, something that had to be taken care of but not something that was necessarily wanted.

When he met and fell in love with his wife and she with him, he had finally realized he was worthy because Aponi thought he was. Once he had come home from Afghanistan, completed nursing school, opened his mind to the world, and stopped being a kid and started being a man, he cut himself some slack. He had a life, friends, family, a job, a business. He was the man, happy-go-lucky, worried about dick. Unfortunately, he fell back to his asshole ways and took them all for granted. He compounded that with acting like a snot-nosed kid and packing up and running away when shit hit the fan.

Now it was time to pay the piper.

His motorcycle boots sounded muted but heavy on the wood laminate floors that were all they could afford when they bought the place. He smiled. Aponi had refused to change them out when they finally could have bought hardwood. She said that she knew where all the cracks and nicks were, how to hide them with rugs or Magic Marker, and she didn't want to spend any time fretting about scratching expensive flooring.

There it was—the only piece of furniture left Rhonda had not sold, traded, or given away. The round kitchen table, with the four-footed central base, he and Aponi had spent three weekends stripping, sanding, and staining. The buzzing in his ears was suddenly deafening and he felt a remembered tremor in his legs, just like the one he had felt on a much-enhanced scale the night Jake and John had come to tell him about the shooting at the clinic.

He didn't hit his knees like he did that night. He stepped quickly to the single folding chair that had been left beside the table, and carefully eased his bulk down into it. But his hands were shaking slightly. Fuck. Why did this table have to be here? Fuck. They had finished the table and fucked in the shower afterward. Then she had come back out to the kitchen to admire their work.

"Do you know why I like this table so much? Because it's you. A complete mess until we took the time to clean it up, fix its nicks, and make it beautiful."

She had laughed, so had he. Then he had made love to her again on the kitchen floor.

He bent at the waist, his elbows resting on his knees, the buzzing in his ears reaching a crescendo. Then, just like that, it was gone. He took a deep breath. Nothing. No noise, not even the whir of the central heat Rhonda had left on for him. He took another measured breath. That's when he heard it again, and this time he wasn't anywhere near sleep.

"Uyehi, be happy."

They were so little, no more than two to three months old by her expert estimation. They were probably from the same litter, although their markings were different. Both were a mixture of cream, gray, and orange. One was a female and predominantly a smoky gray in color. The other, a male, was more cream and orange with just ribbons of the same smoky gray. They were not overly plump, but they were not malnourished. Their coats were relatively clean, and she had found no visible wounds or injuries or signs of obvious illness. There were small, narrow, white flea prevention collars around their necks.

The kittens were also quite dead, and judging by the rigor, had been for at least a day or so.

Olivia turned away from the exam table, picked up a roll of medical paper, and tore off a large sheet. She draped it carefully over the two small bodies she had found on the grass under the tree in her front yard when she went out to get her mail. She ground her back molars and turned to the large stainless-steel sink to wash her hands, snapping off the blue surgical gloves as she went.

Days like this were when it royally sucked to be a vet. Days like this when she woke to find a rail-thin, flea-infested, starving German shepherd chained to her back fence. Nights when she was awakened by Snape, raising his deep Newfie bark at the cage full of starving chickens that was somehow on her front porch. She had wanted to be a small animal vet for as long as she could remember, but there were days when she longed to be an accountant.

"Any idea what they died from?" her vet tech, Bryan, asked. When she turned from the sink, she watched as Bryan placed the small furry corpses into the container he would use to prepare them for cremation. Yeah, there were days this job sucked hugely.

Olivia moved to get the disinfectant, in preparation for cleaning down the examination table. "From the petechial hemorrhages, I'd say they asphyxiated. "

The younger man paused on his way out with the small container. "Shit. I wonder how it happened. Where did you say you found them?"

"They were out in the front yard, under that tree by the mailbox, side by side." She put on fresh gloves and started the cleanup. "Somebody must have put them out there last night after I locked up and went to bed."

The tech turned and pushed the swinging door that led to the outer clinic open. "Shit."

He went out the door and Olivia took the few instruments she had used to examine the kittens to the sink that was next to her autoclave, in preparation for cleaning and sterilization. Shit was right. How did two apparently healthy kittens die from asphyxiation? The flea collars signaled that someone cared at least perfunctorily for them. If their deaths had been accidental, why bring them to the vet's office? Had they been alive when they were left? Jesus, people did shit that made absolutely no sense to her, especially when it came to animals.

Today's event had her feeling creeped out, and she wasn't a person who got creeped out easily. She hadn't slept particularly well, so she put the unease down to fatigue, and the fact she watched too much scary shit on Netflix. It was also coming on winter and a cold front had hit overnight, with clouds covering the stars, and howling wind swerving around the corners of the big house. Olivia was not a huge fan of cold weather, and her childhood home could be a haunted house prototype in the right weather setting.

The picturesque antebellum mini mansion had been built in the 1840s. Like most homes of the era, it had beauty and horror within its walls and history. It was modernized and had been meticulously maintained by her father. The entire bottom floor was the veterinary clinic and was accessible at both sides, as well as from an expansive brick patio at the back of the house. The sweeping front steps bypassed the bottom floor and led directly to a wide covered veranda, adorned with boxes and pots of flowers and greenery. Her father had hired a company to keep the expansive lawn and landscaping looking pristine, but she maintained the porch flora and fauna now herself. Gardening had a way of soothing the mind and spirit, and she loved doing it.

It was Wednesday. She had no clinic hours on Wednesdays, saving that day for the exam rooms and hospital room deep clean, ordering supplies, paying bills, and the never-ending paperwork. It was just gone ten o'clock and she had not had coffee. That was a situation that needed to be addressed immediately. She headed toward the small break room her father had added to the clinic when she came to join the practice.

"Now that you are here, we need to make this place more livable." His kind, quiet voice whispered through her memory, bringing both the smile and the ache that always accompanied it.

There had been no other woman to live there to make it more livable. No other woman to make the clinic, the house, their lives better, softer. No other woman to make her father's life more livable. No other woman came after her mother died because she, Olivia, would not allow it.

"I don't want her here! I don't want her touching my mother's things, cooking in my mother's kitchen. I won't let her sleep in the room where my mother died! And if you bring her here, I'll hate you until the day YOU die!"

Dorothy, the schoolteacher from Maryville her father wanted to marry two years after Olivia's mother died, had never come back to the house after that night. Her father had not remarried. He had died in a hospital bed alone. Olivia didn't get there in time to say goodbye because the heart attack he suffered had been the kind you didn't recover from. He had collapsed on the hardware store floor, in the aisle with the small hand tools. He never regained consciousness. Olivia didn't know it, but the hammer he went there to buy got kicked under a shelf by the paramedics and wasn't found until they remodeled the store last year.

The kittens must have bothered her more than she realized. Emotions unexpectedly overwhelmed her, and she swallowed back the sudden rush of tears that threatened. Entering the small room with the kitchenette and the round table, she sat down heavily in one of the wooden ladder-back chairs. Blowing out a breath, she leaned her head back against the solid wood and closed her eyes. The prickle in her eyes finally subsided. The ever-present, bone-deep sadness ebbed back to its place in her soul. She didn't know what was worse: the feelings of guilt and regret she constantly dragged around or the loneliness that seemed to get worse with each passing day.

Jesus, she was a case. Her headspace was filled with all the supplies required to send her right into middle-aged bitterness, and she had too good a sense of humor for that. Besides, her apple pie was too damn good to wither and die without someone loving her enough to appreciate it. She could hear Mercy Beckett, the town matriarch's voice.

"Life is too short to let the past win, girl."

She needed to go visit Miss Mercy. Olivia was starting to be very afraid that you didn't get to ruin the happiness of two people and get by unscathed.

Breathing deeply and evenly, she sat up straight and fished her cell out of her pocket. She had heard a voicemail ping earlier, during her examination of the kittens. Looking at the screen, she was only mildly curious to see it was an unknown number. Not unheard of since she only hired an answering service to take weekend emergency calls. People called their vets for things both great and small. It was the nature of the job, and she didn't mind it much. It kept her busy.

Pressing the message icon, she put the phone to her ear and looked around for something to write with. She stopped dead when she heard the voice on the phone. It was deep and masculine, with a drawl that was evident but not pronounced.

"Hey, Doc. It's Kyle Valentine. First off, don't call the cops. I finagled your number out of Laura after you left the other night. Listen, I've been worried about your PTSD from my weak-sighted rejection in that parking lot, lo these many years past. What do you say I make it up to you and your therapist by buying you that pizza? Now, to be clear, this is not a date request. It's step one in my recovering asshole program. If you get me past this, I can move on to the next step in my sad moral inventory. So, can you help an asshole out? Just text and let me know so I can plan my groveling accordingly. Friday night, if it works for you."

The click of the disconnect sounded and the automatic recording asking to keep or not to keep sounded, then repeated itself before she recovered from that voice asking for a date. No, it asked for a non-date. She pressed the number to save the message. She saved his number in her phone, not giving herself any time to think and consider before adding him to her contacts.

Then she placed the phone carefully down on the table and stared at it. After taking several breaths, she picked it back up, opened her text screen, and typed. She didn't give herself any wise consideration time before doing that, either.

Kyle

Shaking his head vigorously, Kyle rubbed the gym towel over his head before picking up clean boxer briefs and stepping into them. Now that he was back to managing the Krav Maga studio that bore his last name full time, he was ordering bigger towels. The ones they currently had weren't big enough to dry a Hobbit's ass.

Throwing the inadequate piece of cloth in the direction of the large hamper in the corner of the men's showers, he walked to the door that led out into the locker room. He stopped himself from exiting, walked back to the hamper, and picked up the towel, depositing it inside the large, white bin. Old inconsiderate habits die hard, but they had to die. He was a grown-ass man and the days of expecting someone else to do his dirty work were long past.

He was in a hurry to get to his locker, and he did not bullshit with himself as to the reason. He wanted to check his phone. He had left Olivia Hudson the message that morning. It was now past five o'clock, and he wanted an answer. Patience was a virtue he only had when working with kids, making chili, or fucking. None of those were on the docket for that day.

He yanked the locker open and took the discipline he needed to put on his jeans and the tee shirt he had folded inside. He forced himself to sit down on the bench in front of the lockers and pull on socks and his motorcycle boots. Finally, he reached and grabbed the phone that was in the back corner. He was just about to activate the screen when he stopped himself abruptly and sat back down.

It dawned on him that for the first time in years, he wanted to be with a woman. No, he wanted to be with a specific woman. Not because he was horned up, not because he felt like he should want to, and not because someone told him he should do it. He didn't feel guilty or duplicitous, and that nonfeeling made him uneasy. Shouldn't he feel that anxiety of betrayal? Was he wrong that he had no disquiet in desiring to see and spend time with another woman?

"You're hurting because you love, honey, and if you are capable of love, that capability comes with a bottomless bucket."

He dropped his head and smiled to himself. His aunt, Grace, had a million of those little gems of advice. He was never sure if she made them up or pilfered them from her Bible or her interminable magazines. But when she brought one out, it was usually exactly what you needed to hear, even though you might not want to hear it.

A bottomless bucket.

Bottomless.

He squeezed his eyes shut for a few seconds before he looked down at the phone. Then he swiped to activate the screen. He had a text from her, and he felt like a twelve-year-old when he took a deep breath before opening the message.

"Friday. Seven o'clock. Pick me up in a vehicle with doors. I

would give you the address, but I'm sure Laura already has. If we are attending the Asshole Anonymous meeting afterward, please advise. I may need to rethink my outfit for your gradua-tion ceremony."

He read it twice before throwing back his head and laughing.

Out in the stars, that laughter was heard.

Heard and loved.

Charlie

No, there was not going to be any water. No water, no blanket, no pot to piss in. She was going to feel exactly like those poor little things.

Charlie shuffled through the maze of newspapers, boxes, and garbage bags that led to the bathroom. They followed, crying and mewling.

Tomorrow, lovies. Nothing until tomorrow. But you will eat well before one of you must be sacrificed.

CHAPTER 5: THE PORCH

Olivia

Snape's deep bark sounded and was closely followed by the old-fashioned chimes of the front doorbell. Olivia skated her gaze over her reflection one more time and turned to the door from her bedroom out into the hall. Good jeans, the leather boots, her one and only cashmere sweater, her long hair in a braid over her shoulder; it all looked fine. She also had on good underwear and didn't examine too closely why she had fussed about that.

She was ready and he was here. Nervous butterflies made their presence known in the region of her stomach, and she did her best to ignore them. It was just a date. Not even that, really. It was an unnecessary apology, as he said, not a date. Irrespective of the joking flirtatiousness of his phone message, she knew that huge or insignificant, unrealized apologies clung to you like unwanted balls of lint. Kyle Valentine wanted to make amends for something that happened over twenty years ago. Why was not precisely clear, but given how many unrealized apologies she herself had, she wasn't going to judge him for wanting to make one.

If she got a meal and a few laughs out of the deal of the day, so much the better. But that was where it was fated to end. She had not forgotten she was choosing to spend time with a man who had wooed, married, and lost a woman who had been, by all accounts, the love of his life. There was no denying the man was funny, hot, and intriguing. But there was also no refuting that Olivia needed to be the love of someone's life. She knew herself well enough to know that to settle for less would be something she would not be able to do. She had witnessed some of the stark evidence of his loss and the impact of it. Kyle had shared a relationship with his wife that was rare and having the capacity and desire to find it twice was rarer still.

But my father did it. I destroyed it, but my father found someone to love and who loved him.

The doorbell sounded again, and Snape barked louder and whined. The big black and white dog came to her as she walked down the hallway and into the large front room. He stayed close as she crossed the polished wood floor to the wide front door, with the lead crystal cutouts. She reached and laid her hand on his massive, black head.

"Shhhhh, boy. Enough."

She reached the door and turned slightly to the dog. You didn't have an animal that weighed over one hundred and thirty pounds and not have the ability to control it. Snape was meticulously trained, even if he was the gentlest soul she had ever encountered. He immediately sat at her side. She could feel his big, powerful body lean slightly against her thigh, his attitude still tense and alert. He wasn't a guard dog, but that did not mean he was not protective. He also was more than a little excited at the thought of head scratches and love from whoever was at the door. Snape was an attention whore in the purest sense of the term. Raising her hand, palm out toward the dog's solemn, serious doggy face, she gave two more commands.

"Sit, boy. Stay."

The massive black and white Newfoundland sat and stayed, but she knew he wasn't happy about it. Peering through the prisms of the crystal glass in the door, she couldn't make out the person standing there's features, but she could tell it was a man, a big man. No going back now. Reaching to the doorknob, she pulled the heavy oak door open and surveyed her gentleman caller, as it were.

Oddly, neither one of them spoke for a full five seconds, as the each took inventory of the other. She casually eyed him from the shoulders up. He surveyed her from the floor up. His look wasn't leering, but it was shameless and appreciative. It was accompanied by a grin that fortunately went all the way across his face to include his eyes. She could see a black leather jacket with zippers and pockets, though finer details were hidden in the dim porch light. Under it he had on a black button-down shirt and what looked like a white thermal showing through the open collar.

Nice.

"Will I do?" The grin also showed in his voice. It was

deep, of course, but teasing and light. "Because I gotta tell ya, Doc, we might need to have a serious conversation about that sweater."

Olivia backed up, pulling the door wide so he could enter. Snape was where she had told him to stay, but his tail was thumping, and he was panting with the need to come greet the new arrival. Kyle stepped through the door and into her house, passing close. A faint scent of clean male cologne and cold outdoors came in with him.

Very nice.

He glanced at her before immediately stepping toward her dog. "Am I going to get eaten if I try to make friends?"

She moved to close the door on the night and the chill in the air. "Only if you have cheese or bacon hidden in the pockets of that jacket, which we might need to include in our wardrobe discussion." If he could initiate a flirt, she certainly could volley. Besides, that jacket was the male equivalent of fuck-me shoes, as far as she was concerned.

She watched as the towering man bent his body in half to squat in front of her dog. He didn't just briefly rub the giant furball's head. She felt a slight hiccup in her breathing when he put his big hands on either side of the dog's furry neck and began to massage. Then his voice sent her respiratory rate spiraling. The tone he used when he spoke to Snape sounded completely different than any she had heard thus far from the man. It was deep, quiet, and caressing in its affectionate appreciation.

"Hey there, big guy. Hey there. What's your name? Damn, you're just gorgeous, aren't you?"

Swallowing with some difficulty, Olivia turned toward her coatrack and endeavored to get her equilibrium back. The thought of him ever talking to her, like he was presently crooning to her dog, had suddenly taken up permanent residence in her fantasy file. Taking her coat and scarf off the antique coatrack beside the door, she pushed her arms through the sleeves of the navy blue peacoat and wrapped the cream scarf that matched her sweater around her neck. Stepping back to the other side of the door, she took several measured breaths.

This would not do. It was just pizza. She needed to get him away from her dog and out of her house, because men who liked dogs were a weakness for her, and she didn't need anything else to make Kyle Valentine more attractive.

Kyle

He wasn't trying to like her. He wasn't trying to find her interesting or funny or subtly sexy. He hadn't anticipated that she would give back as good as she got. But fuck him—everything about her was good. She didn't apologize for the occasional obscenity. She responded to his bullshitting easily, but without being measured or calculating. She laughed out loud, she ate pizza with her hands, and that goddamn sweater was going to be giving him wet dreams for a month.

Things hadn't gotten serious or heavy until he had spoken a reference to Aponi. He did this occasionally. He had spent years with the woman, lived his life with her, and there had been a lot of life. He naturally referred to her in conversation. He had no problem with it. It was just like anyone referencing their close family and friends. The only time it went south was when he mentioned her and the person he was talking to had a sphincter spasm. Or, as was much more common, when he sensed it made people uncomfortable to talk about the dead. He knew that, but there was really nothing he could do except be cognizant and try not to make it weird or uncomfortable. He knew most of the time people were afraid of making him feel sad, and that alone helped him to police his conversations.

Kyle had long ago come to an uneasy peace with the reality of loss and dying. He had been a field medic in the military and a nurse for many years. For him, death was as near the surface as living was for most. In his work, he had of necessity learned to not let the Reaper win, either in flesh or spirit, any more than he had to.

Aponi and her Cherokee heritage had embraced the acceptance of all that was existence. Aponi had taught him about balance and order. Some of it warred with the angels and demons in his head, and he fought those fights. In the last year or so, he won more than he lost, and because of her he had a peace in his soul about most things. Losing her was the greatest battle he had ever waged with his baser side. The irony was, having her ultimately made it easier to accept losing her. Life was some fucked-up shit sometimes.

He knew the reasons for coming back to Faithful. He needed to win this last battle so the war could be over. He wanted to make amends to those who loved him and who he loved. He needed to tie up loose ends, clean out the proverbial garage, and move the fuck on.

However, casually bringing up his dead wife's name while he was on a date, might not signal he had his gargantuan pile of shit exactly all in one hemisphere. It happened when they were eating dessert. She had ordered cannoli. He had the tiramisu. She had given him a mild portion of shit about his order.

Eyeing his plate, she remarked, "Nothin' but love for the Italian people, but soaking stale cake in coffee strong enough to walk onto the plate by itself is not exactly my idea of dessert."

He watched her grin and noticed, in addition to those freckles, she also had a dimple in her left cheek.

"Well, damn." He thought. *"Just what I need—freckles and a fucking dimple."*

She watched him slice into his dessert. She kept her eyes on him while taking one of the cylinders of cannoli and biting into it, the shell crumbling in her hand. He watched her, nearly laughing out loud at her struggle to save the demolished sweet. She finally managed to place the rest of the dessert on her plate and deal with the monstrous portion in her mouth. He tried to be a gentleman and not call attention to her predicament. He failed because she just looked too damn cute trying to maintain her dignity. He spoke before he weighed his words.

"Aponi once told me that eating cannoli was like eating cold snot in an old cracker tube."

He grinned and leaned over, pulled a napkin out of the holder on the wooden table, and wiped the side of her face like she was a child. He looked into her eyes and his hand stilled with the napkin touching the side of her mouth. Shit. Why did he say that? Now she would pull back and go into "let's make the poor widower feel better" mode.

Only she didn't. She just looked into his eyes for several seconds, then reached up and took the napkin from his hand. She finished the wipe up and he returned his own hand to his side of the table. But she didn't stop looking into his eyes. Hers were gray and blue and some green, the color of an ocean lagoon in the Pacific. He couldn't decipher the expressions that flitted through them. There might have been a flash of sympathy, of concern, but he didn't see discomfort and he didn't detect pity, thank Christ.

Then she smiled, and it was a genuine smile of warm humor before she said words that made him ease and stemmed the flow of regret about mentioning Aponi's name.

"She was right. I can just tolerate snot better than bad coffee, and I gotta have something sweet after pizza."

Just like that, everything was okay. The dinner was okay, dessert, harmless flirting, and talking about his boat and her job was okay. The attraction he felt was okay, in large part because he felt she was okay with it too. He was no kid, and she was no teenager. He felt the warmth in her hand when he helped her down out of the pickup, and he also felt the spark. He had not called her because he needed to make up for a pizza, and she did not wear that sweater because she was cold. There was interest and attraction on both sides.

They were at her front door, where two radiant carriage lights cast the porch in a dim but warm glow, when the easy silence that had permeated the ride home was broken. She didn't reach for keys but instead turned to face him.

"Thank you. I had a really good time, regardless of the cannoli."

He watched her mouth as she smiled up at him. He was going to get a taste of those lips, and he did not give one single fuck about propriety. But he had to know if she wanted that too. So instead of firing up his timeworn arsenal of "hey baby, let's get to it" moves, he simply looked at her.

As he stood in the shadows of her porch saying goodnight, he allowed himself to really see her face. He loved those damn freckles that danced across her nose and on to her cheekbones. He didn't feel guilt for admiring them. He didn't feel unease because something he found beautiful was on the face of another woman. He felt warmth in his gut and in his groin and he sensed them without remorse, for there was nothing to be remorseful for. Those small, brown flecks on her face were a gift to him, and by God, he was going to accept them. He was going to go after them because doing so was right, and because he had enough room to take them in.

"I like freckles."

Her head tilted slightly to the side and she frowned up at him. "You do?"

He raised a hand and slid his forefinger down from

the slight crease between her brows, across the bridge of her nose, pausing at her cheek.

Her skin was soft.

Silky.

Warm.

"Yeah. They make you look like you enjoy making trouble." He moved his hand until his finger was near the corner of her mouth. "I'm all for a little trouble."

She didn't respond, but she didn't move away either. He could feel her breath on his arm from her slightly parted lips, and it was coming faster. He slid his finger across her bottom lip, stopping in the middle and pulling down ever so slightly.

"You like trouble, Olivia Mae?" He pushed his finger just beyond the barrier of her teeth. She let him, and he stepped closer. She let him do that, too.

"My tongue really wants to be down your throat right now." He felt his own respiratory rate escalating. Oh, fuck yeah, he wanted his tongue on her and in her; in lots of ways and in lots of places. But he'd start with her mouth.

His dick leapt in his jeans when he felt the tip of her tongue slide across the pad of his finger. Quick as a wink it was gone, but then her hands were on him at his chest.

"Far be it from me to disappoint."

When he was a younger man, a situation like this would have progressed with him moving in, taking what he wanted, escalating an already hot situation. He would have gone at it until he got a feel, or a taste, or a fuck. He wasn't going to shit himself. He wanted all that and more from her. But not just there and not just then.

So instead of falling on her like a horned-up frat boy, he brought his other hand up to cup the back of her head, sliding his fingers into the silk of her hair. The hand that had been on her lips moved to grasp her face gently but firmly, his fingers gripping the curve of her jaw. He held her like that for a moment and looked into her eyes, and he knew what she knew.

This was no simple goodnight kiss on a porch. It was something else, and he knew it.

"Here we go, Olivia Mae," he whispered.

CHAPTER 6: A MESS IN THE KITCHEN

Olivia

"Here we go, Olivia Mae."

His deep voice whispered the words and a nanosecond later his mouth opened over her lips, his tongue slipping past the barrier of her teeth. Big hands held the back of her head and firmly to her jaw; positioning her head at the angle he wanted. His mouth wasn't tentative, but neither was it aggressive. He moved his lips and tongue firmly and surely. The man knew what he was doing, no doubt. But with the obvious skill there was tenderness. His hands on her were strong but gentle, his tongue probed but light, sweet, and delicious. She parted her lips wider for him, offering her mouth for the dance.

And dance they did.

For long moments they simply tasted each other, her hands flat on his chest as he held her. She could not stop a small moan when he moved the hand from her jaw to the side of her face, adjusting the fingers of both hands in order to hold her face still as he drew her closer, until her hands were crushed between them. She nipped the tip of his tongue and was satisfied by the answering groan that came from low in his throat.

She froze as that groan registered low in her belly. Heat radiated through her body. Okay, time to get a grip. She pulled her head back against his hold. She didn't make the movement forceful, but she made it clear she wanted to break the kiss. He followed her lead, moving his own head back. He didn't let her go, though. Instead she watched closely as he smiled with that same hint of wicked she had glimpsed more than once.

"Well, well, well." He held her eyes with his. His voice was deeper than its normal gravelly timbre.

Her own voice was unsteady and husky. "Indeed."

He took a slight step back and slid his hands to either side of her neck. "That, as they say in jolly old England, was quite brilliant. Any chance we can do it again, right now? I sense you might need a minute." His voice was teasing, and she grinned back up at him as she steadied her equilibrium.

"You think your skill and finesse is that overwhelming, huh?" she teased back.

His eyes sparkled with humor as he replied, "I think my brash confidence and your obvious talent level make what just happened the *American Idol* winner of smooches, so you need a minute to collect yourself."

His palms slid down her shoulders and back to rest at her waist, and she moved her own hands to rest on his massive forearms. The supple leather beneath her fingers did little to hide the power of his embrace. He was so big, so powerful, so *much* it was intimidating, even in their current situation. Olivia was not what would be termed petite, yet she felt dwarfed by his size and his personality. It wasn't in a bad way, but it was a lot to take in, especially since he had just given her a kiss that literally left her barely able to breathe. He was right. She needed a minute, or ten, to adjust herself.

She did not, however, want the night to end. She was not going to sleep with him on a first date. No way was she ready for that. But she wanted more of his kisses and his company. It could not be denied. She could play the game as the usual rules warranted, or she could just be honest. So, she took a breath and spoke her mind.

"If I invite you in to have a drink and a cookie, or whatever I can scrounge up out of my kitchen, can we make the understanding now that the invitation does not include you seeing my bedspread?"

She watched as his smile faded and a look she couldn't interpret moved into his eyes. Just like at the cookout, she was struck by the fact he projected a devil may care, smart-ass bravado effortlessly. The juxtaposition was it frequently did not match with what was going on behind his expression. Right then, he wasn't even trying to play the smart-ass. He was quiet and looked at her for several seconds before he spoke, his voice gentle but more serious than the words might have indicated.

"I would love to have a cookie or a pickle or whatever is not expired in your fridge. I would also really love to sit on a couch next to you and play with your mouth until I am forced to leave by my good manners and better judgment." His grin reappeared, but his eyes were gentle and warm. "No bedspread tonight, Olivia Mae."

Her heart skipped at the nickname and the warmth in his eyes. She regarded him for a moment longer, then she turned from his arms, and slid the key into the lock of the door.

Please don't make me regret this. Please don't make me regret this.

Kyle

He was frankly shocked she had invited him inside. As he followed her into her comfortable living room, he replayed the conversation they just had. Okay, he hadn't asked to come in. She had asked him. She was completely honest about what was and what was not going to happen. He liked she didn't play games, that she was forthright and open about what she did and did not want.

There had been a day, many of them, in fact, where he would have bullshitted, told the woman whatever she wanted to hear, then made a full-court press to get him some pussy. He was not proud of it. Back before Aponi, on the rare occasion that it happened, Kyle had never taken the first "no" as a firm answer. He had never forced himself on a woman; he hadn't had to. But there had been more than one time when he had used charm and pressure to get what he wanted from a woman. He had told Aponi once when they were dating to "Smile, baby."

He had been informed with lightning speed, and in no uncertain terms, never to do it again. Afterward he had learned over the course of the years of their relationship how much women had to put up with just to exist in the world. It had shamed him, and he made a vow that if or when they had kids, they would be taught by word and example how to treat each other—boys and girls. Over time Kyle had observed his wife and other women he cared about navigate life in continuous combat mode. It fundamentally shifted something inside him.

Now, standing here with Olivia, he did a quick mental inventory to make sure he had not and did not do anything to make her feel uncomfortable. He must have stood in the entryway so long that it got weird, because she turned from her position by one of the couches that furnished the room, and looked quizzically at him before reaching out a hand and beckoning slightly.

"You can hang your jacket there by the door and come on in. I'm going to go let Snape in off the porch. He likes being out there when it's cold." She walked past the couch and indicated it with a sweep of her arm. "Sit down and get comfortable. Would you like beer or iced tea?" She moved through a cased opening in the wall that led to a hallway. He could see a set of swinging doors beyond. That must have been the kitchen.

He had his jacket off and was turning to hang it when she screamed.

It wasn't a screech, like she just stepped on a spider. It wasn't an exclamation like she had seen a mouse. It was a scream of sheer horror and shock. In two steps he was at the kitchen doors where she stood holding one side of the double entry open with a hand, the other hand pressed to her mouth to stifle another scream. Kyle pushed open the other door. The sight beyond the doors stopped him dead.

The streaks and slashes of red were everywhere. It marred the lower doors of the white, distressed cabinets, the bottom half of the old-fashioned fridge-freezer, the oven doors of the antique stove. It has been slung so that the frilly curtains with cherries on them, covering the window in the door at the side of the room, had droplets staining them. The gleaming pine floors and the scattered kitchen rugs were standing in pools of it.

Then there was the island.

In the middle of the spacious room with the hanging copper pots, and the built-in china cabinet with Olivia's grandmother's collection of Haviland china, was a heavy wooden island of the same distressed white oak as the cabinets. There were shelves and drawers with antique glass knobs. The legs were heavy and carved with vines and flowers. There was a cutout that held a collection of what was most likely cookbooks. They would all have to be replaced now, of course.

They would have to be replaced because of what was on the top of its worn butcher block. Kyle felt bile rise in his throat, and that took a lot, considering what he had seen in his life. But what lay before him was right up there with his top five list of shit that would give him bad dreams for a while. It was the carcass of a medium-sized dog. It could have been some sort of shepherd, but it was hard to tell. The animal had been gutted where it lay, gore running off the butcher block and onto the shelves below. Rivulets of blood were still dripping onto the floor that surrounded the island. It looked like the scene in a B-rated slasher film.

Unfortunately, it was real and right before his eyes. It crossed his mind for a second that maybe it was all fake. But he knew it wasn't. The animal's eyes were open and dull; the smell in the room was nauseating—metallic and vile. The air was thick with the scent of feces and death, and he swallowed thickly. *Holy fuck, who had done this?* Hard on the heels of that thought was the concern that whoever had done this might still be in the house. He turned abruptly as his instincts kicked in, and he reached for Olivia with one hand and to his pocket for his phone with the other. He heard her repeat the words, "Oh, God, Oh, God" as he pulled her around.

"Come on, baby. Come on, Livie," he crooned in a soft voice.

He needed to get her out of that room. He needed to get her safe. He had to check the house, and he had to call Sam. Sam Beckett was the chief of police and they needed the cops *right motherfuckin' now*. But first he had to get her out of there and away from that blasphemous scene currently occupying her kitchen. He had her turned around, and halfway to the front door, when she suddenly gave her arm a mighty yank from his grasp and turned back to the opening.

"Olivia, no!" He shoved his phone back and twisted to catch her, to stop her from going back into that kitchen. But she turned to the left abruptly at the hall and he swerved to follow her. His steps became a jog because she was running, the heels of her boots pounding into the wooden floors

"Stop, honey! Olivia, stop!" She sped up, took a right turn, and disappeared. He heard the deep bark before he could get to the door that was located at the end of the hall and to the right. He rounded the corner, and he was in a large screened in porch, dim shadows indicating there was furniture scattered around. Olivia was already on her knees, her arms wrapped around the big black and white Landseer Newfoundland that was barking and giving low growls

She was repeating the words again, over, and over. "Oh, God, Oh, God, Oh, God."

Kyle made a quick inspection of the room. French doors that likely opened outside onto the porch were closed. Moonlight showed that the furniture appeared to be in place, and there was no immediate evidence anyone had disturbed the room. He turned, searching, and flipped a switch at the side of the door leading to the interior of the house. Two table lamps switched on, bathing the room in cozy lighting.

The room was empty of life but the big dog currently woofing and whining as Olivia held him, rocking back and forth. Kyle assessed his options and decided to call Sam first. The house was huge, and if the person who had done what had been done in the kitchen were still in it, he'd worry about it when he had backup who had weaponry. He could handle himself very efficiently against attack, but it had required a hefty tool with a sharp blade to do what had been done in that kitchen, and the mindset to do it necessitated batshit crazy. Therefore, he was going to get reinforcements.

He pushed a contact on his cell and squatted down

on the tile floor next to Olivia and Snape, pushing the door to the main house shut as he went. He could hear her softly crooning to the dog, telling him he was a good boy, telling him everything was going to be okay. Slipping his free hand up her back to rest at the nape of her neck, he lifted the phone to his ear. He heard the ring and waited. The call was picked up before the second ring.

"Faithful Police Department. Valentine." The no-shit voice of Aunt Rhonda sounded clearly through the connection.

"Rhon, it's Kyle. I need a car and Sam out at Olivia Hudson's house. Now."

There was barely a fraction of a second of hesitation before her clipped, no-nonsense voice came back. "You okay?"

A part of him felt the concern from the woman who had been his mother since almost before he could remember. But he didn't have time to go there with her; therefore, his voice was as clipped as her question had been.

"Yeah. But there's been a break-in here, and I can't search to see if the asshole is still on the premises. I need a couple of uniforms and Sam, and I need them yesterday. Got it?"

There was no hesitation this time. "Got it. Location? As I recall, that's a big-ass house."

He felt Olivia's attention on him. She didn't speak and she didn't move, her hands still holding on to her dog. "Tell them to proceed with caution and come around to the back and upstairs to the screened-in porch. We are both here." He turned his face from the phone to Olivia. "Is there anyone else here, baby? Working in the clinic, anything?"

He watched as she struggled to focus for a moment. Her eyes met his. "No. I don't have any overnights in the clinic today."

He turned his attention back to the phone but squeezed her neck lightly. He could feel her body trembling slightly, and he knew the aftershocks of what they had seen were about to set in for her.

"There shouldn't be anyone else in the house or clinic, so tell the boys and Sam if they see anybody, they need to be contained. Gotta go. Get 'em here, Rhon."

He didn't wait for a reply. He hit the screen on the phone and shoved it into his pocket. He sat down on the cold floor beside Olivia and put both arms around her, gently loosening her hold on the dog. She came without a fight, her body starting to shake harder.

"Kyle..." Her voice was unsteady.

"I'm here, baby."

"Oh, God, oh God, Kyle...in my house..." Her voice broke and he felt every muscle in her body start to quake.

He clenched his jaw so hard he could have cracked a tooth. "You're safe, honey. The cops are on the way. I've got you. It's gonna be all right. I've got you."

He sat on the floor of her porch with cold seeping into his ass, holding her in his arms, with her dog's head on her lap, until Sam Beckett called to say he was coming into the house. He repeated the words over and over, and she let him.

He kept his mind occupied with practical things,

even as he kept his senses alert for any minute sound that didn't belong. But under it, his temper was boiling. Some psycho fucker was going to regret the day he was born for making this woman feel like this, for violating her home. He started also to sort the questions. Who did this? Why? How did they get in? Again, why would anyone do this sick shit to her? What would have happened if she had been at home?

That was the one that made his blood chill in his veins. She could have been here. She could have been confronted by the psycho.

He felt the trembling in her body fade a little and the tears let loose. Good. She needed the release. His outlet would come when he got his hands on the sick fuck who had gutted a dog in the middle of her kitchen.

Charlie

Charlie scrubbed with the boar bristle brush until the underside of both arms were bleeding.

"Gotta stay clean. That's what your mama didn't understand. You always gotta be clean." The voice echoed thru the huge bathroom. "That's why she left, you know. She couldn't stand being clean."

Charlie scrubbed until the dark blood from the poor thing stopped sliding down the drain, and the water was only tinged pink with the new that seeped from the places where the brush had gotten past the surface of skin.

<hr>

CHAPTER 7: ONE BIG COSTCO TRIP

Olivia

<hr>

One minute she was asleep, the next she was sitting up in the unfamiliar bed, gasping at the images of the dream, her breathing hard, and her heart pounding. Snape woofed from somewhere on the floor. She was confused and struggled to orient herself. Okay, the dream was just that—a dream. Okay. She closed her eyes and attempted to regulate her respiratory rate. She took two deep breaths, opened her eyes, and it all came rushing back at once: the kitchen, the blood, the cops.

And Kyle.

Kyle, who had held her on the floor of her porch until Sam Beckett arrived in a flurry of sirens, his police badge clipped to his belt, in lieu of a uniform, at ten o'clock at night. It was Kyle who had dealt with Sam and the other two police officers, showing Sam and the male officer the kitchen while the female officer, Tammy, had stayed with her and Snape on the porch. It was Kyle who brought her a bottle of water from the small fridge on the patio, and it was him who had sat close on the patio sofa while Sam asked her the questions.

Did she have anyone who wished her ill?

Did she have any idea who would or could do such a thing?

Had she had any unusual phone calls or mail or visitors or clients?

How was someone able to get into her house without signs of a break-in?

That one had been easy enough. She had forgotten to lock the side door that let out onto the wraparound veranda, again. The side door led into the butler's pantry and from there through into the kitchen. It was unlocked more than it was locked, and in her neighborhood—indeed, in Faithful itself—going to bed with an unlocked door was not uncommon. Snape had probably barked twice and decided it was not his job to care about someone coming into the house. The dog's chief interests in life were food and if he was going to be allowed up on Olivia's bed at night. Those and a good swim every now and then were the extent of her dog's concerns.

She vaguely remembered Sam muttering that there had been no sign of forced entry anywhere. There was also no evidence the perpetrator had been elsewhere in the house. As for his other questions, Olivia had no clue who might have defiled her home. The closest she got to having enemies was when she confronted someone who had mistreated an animal, but she usually reported that to the police. It happened, not frequently, but it happened. Most of that kind of thing occurred in hoarding situations, which she sometimes volunteered her services to aid with when the animals were found and rescued.

That was it. That was the extent of her brushes with unsavory citizens. It made no sense, what had been done. Why would anyone enact such craziness? Who would want to do such a thing to her? Snape woofed and startled her out of her trance of questions. That was when she remembered the rest of the night, or what had been left of it when the police and crime scene people had left.

While various and sundry people went in and out of her house, their footsteps echoing down the hall, she sat on the sofa close to Kyle. He got up one or twice to go out and presumably direct traffic and answer questions. But for most of the hours it took for the police to process the scene, he sat beside her on the narrow wicker loveseat. He asked her once if she needed anything, and twice if she was doing okay. He kept a muscled arm along the back of the seat behind her, but he didn't touch her.

No, that wasn't exactly right. He touched her once. He moved his arm to circle her shoulders tightly when Sam had asked her to walk him through exactly what she had seen and heard when she went into the kitchen. Reliving it less than an hour after it happened had been almost as awful as going through it the first time. She was compelled to replay the pictures, re-smell the odor, rewind the film in her head repeatedly as Sam gently, but forcefully, questioned her. While she reexperienced it again in all the excruciating, Technicolor detail that the investigation required, she felt Kyle's strength surrounding her frame. It felt good and right and reassuring. When Sam had deferred questions to him, Kyle had answered in a low, calm, and steady voice, and all the time his presence next to her had made the ordeal more bearable.

For her part, Olivia had felt like she was in a daze, like the world around her was part of some other space-time continuum where she did not belong. She heard herself speaking, but it sounded like it came from someone outside of her being. A part of her mind kept seeing the blood and the animal on the island where she spread jam on her biscuits and rolled out her piecrusts.

By the time Sam was finished with questions and discussion, it was past one o'clock in the morning. She had fallen silent as the two men debated possibilities and theories in low tones. The echoes of people going in and out of the house had ceased. She was exhausted and thoughts of how and what she needed to do to return her home to a clean, safe place had started to bombard her brain. The fallout from the adrenaline overload was crashing, and she wanted to sleep and not wake up until it was all fixed. Except, she could not sleep in that house, not tonight, and maybe not for a while.

She moved to slide her hand into the pocket of her jeans for her phone. It was a drive, but she would have to hit the Holiday Inn out by the interstate. Faithful had two hotels and neither was in the town itself, but out on the county roads that connected the main travel highways. She brought her phone out and hit the screen, searching for phone numbers. Laura and Jake would no doubt let her spend a few days with them, but no way was she waking them at this hour.

"What are you doing, Liv?" Kyle's voice was still quiet and low.

She scrolled and perused the screen, not looking up at him. If she looked up at him, she might fall apart, and she did not have time for that. She could feel herself hanging by a slim thread and those eyes, filled with concern, would undo her.

"I'm looking for the number of a hotel so I can get a room for the next couple of days, until I can fix the house."

This was not an entirely true statement. She wasn't fixing the house. She was going to be lucky if she could bring herself to ever set foot in that kitchen again. After she slept for sixteen hours, she was going to hire someone, several someones, to clean, fumigate, and perform an exorcism on her house. Then she was going to research how to apply for an equity loan so she could demolish the kitchen down to the studs and rebuild it. She was going to do this after she went to Costco and bought approximately seven hundred gallons of bleach, in order to douse the entire place.

But first she needed somewhere to sleep for a few days. Now if she could just remember how to spell 'holiday.' A big hand came into her line of sight and took her phone out of her hands.

"I've got two bedrooms. You can stay at my place."

He sounded matter-of-fact, like it was the obvious

thing for him to say and for her to do. She looked up at him silently. At another time, and in other circumstances, she would have demurred, argued, made excuses and reasons, and refused. She did not have it in her to do any of that just then. Relief flooded her and for the first time in more years than she could count, she simply let herself be taken care of.

"Okay."

She whispered the word as she looked at him. She saw surprise cross his face for a second, but he didn't give her any time to back out. He stood then reached down, took her hand, and pulled her up from the seat.

"Let's go get whatever you need. Is your bedroom one of the doors off the hallway?"

It was and she didn't even have the energy to think about Kyle Valentine being in her bedroom. She just let him lead her into it. He asked and she told him where her overnight bags were, which clothes were in which drawers. She sat on the edge of her bed, holding on to Snape who jumped up beside her. She didn't react as he packed her a bag. She didn't care what he was seeing or touching. She had started to shake again, her teeth chattering slightly, and she held on to her dog like a life preserver in a storm at sea.

When he was finished packing to his satisfaction, he went back into her closet for the final time and came out with a heavy suede jacket. Silently he took one of her hands and pulled her up to stand in front of him. He held her jacket for her like she was a five-year-old child and moved her arms into the sleeves. The only time he spoke was to ask if Snape was good off lead, and she had shuddered jerkily and said yes.

The leashes were hanging by the china cabinet in the kitchen.

He led her and her dog back out onto the screened in patio, past the furniture and the pots of plants, through the French doors, and out onto the wraparound veranda. He steered them the long way around, away from the corner where the kitchen was, and down the front steps to his big black pickup with the double cab.

When he had her and Snape inside, he maneuvered his big body into the driver's seat. He hesitated before he started the truck, and she moved her attention from looking out the side window away from the house to him.

"Doin' okay?" He asked the question like they had just finished a day at the beach.

She nearly laughed hysterically.

"Do you need an honest answer to that?" Her voice was shaky.

Reaching a long arm across the expanse of leather seat, he took one of her icy hands in his. His touch was warm and strong and solid. "Nope. Lie to me. I like beautiful women who lie to me. Makes me feel secure of my place in the world."

Amazingly she nearly smiled.

"I'm ducky. Hakuna matata." Her voice sounded less flat.

He squeezed her hand, released it, and moved to start the truck. "Good. Can't have you throwing up in my new dick wagon."

He drove her to his house, stopping to get dog food at a convenience store along the way. He showed her where the spare bedroom and guest bathroom were, put down a bowl of water for Snape, and told her good night at the door of the room. He didn't initiate any further conversation, and he didn't touch her again. When she crawled between the sheets in the spare room, she realized she hadn't had any more shaking episodes.

***

Now here she sat in that bed, the factory creases still visible in the sheets and blanket that covered her. The window had light creeping in through plain white mini blinds. There were no curtains, and nothing hung on the pale green walls. The room was furnished with the bed she slept in, which she recognized as new because there were still brand tags hanging from the headboard. There was a small bedside table that looked like it might be plastic, with a cheap, black, ginger jar lamp on top. Beside the lamp, and taking up the remainder of the tabletop surface, was a pile of fluffy black towels and a washcloth that was still tied in the black ribbon they had been purchased with. A huge, worn, Mission-style wooden rocking chair took up one corner. Idly she wondered how long he'd had that chair, since it clearly did not belong in the functional but economical and plain room. She didn't know much about how Kyle had lived in the last years, but she did know it had been on a boat. There was no way that chair had ever fit on a boat, unless it was a Dubai-sized yacht. She also wondered when he had brought the towels in. It made her uncomfortable to know he had seen her sleeping.

The room had a pristine clean, never-been-lived-in aura. It smelled like new fabric, fresh paint, newly sanded wood, and lemony cleaner. Looking over the foot of the bed, she saw Snape was stretched out on a circular area rug that was too small to contain all of him. His thick, sturdy legs with the webbed toes hung off the side. He had woofed when she woke so suddenly, but he was currently back to doggy dreamland.

She was continuing her perusal of the space and trying to remember where she had left her phone, when there was a brief knock on the door. She looked down at herself. Kyle had packed a pair of flannel pajamas for her that she had last worn a year or more ago. They were more than decent, and the tiny pink and blue flowers covering them would have been appropriate for Olivia's grandmother when she was alive. They had been obtained for a sleepover at Laura Beckett's house, bought as ordered by the hostess, to be worn while they got totally drunk and watched *Downton Abbey*. She hadn't worn them since because they were flannel, hot, and restrictive. She preferred sleepwear that was briefer and more voluminous.

The second knock was louder and longer.

She swallowed. "Come in."

Kyle

He should have been prepared to see her this morning. It should have been nothing monumental. After the events of the night before, and after dealing with what he had dealt with that morning, he should have been too ass-dragging tired and preoccupied to notice anything about the woman in the bed in front of him.

Come to find out, he wasn't that tired. Not so tired he didn't notice her bed hair and wonder if she looked like that after sex. Not so preoccupied he didn't wonder what she had on under those granny jammies that somehow made her look sexy as all fuck. Definitely not too beat to notice her cheeks with no makeup, her freckles unmasked for him, and her eyes, that blue-green of a shallow island lagoon.

Damn. He was gonna start spouting poetry if he didn't get a grip. Fuck him, she was pretty. He really, really wanted to kiss her again. What he did not want to do was talk about last night. But he wasn't going to get what he wanted. He would have to wait to taste that mouth again, and he couldn't ignore what lay before her simply because he wanted to protect her and/or make out with her.

He had been up only a couple of hours after he went to bed, and on the phone for the last hour and a half. He had driven the couple of miles to her house and checked the outside. The doors and windows had been secure. He hadn't gone back inside, because he frankly didn't want to see that scene in broad daylight. He'd talked to Sam, and he'd talked to her vet tech. He'd contacted the home cleaning and restoration service, and he'd talked to Laura Beckett. Then he came back, made the coffee in the cup he held, toasted the bagel he currently carried on a plate, along with a banana, which was all he had in the way of breakfast. Now he was here, looking at her sitting in a bed in the rental house he had only been living in for a couple of weeks, and his uppermost thought was of sticking his tongue down her throat.

Jesus.

"So," he said, walking over and handing her the cup and the plate. "What do you want to do today?"

Fuck him, she was gorgeous when she smiled.

CHAPTER 8: PSYCHOS AND BLOW JOBS

Kyle

She took the coffee and instantly put the cup to her lips, blowing slightly then taking a sip. She closed her eyes in a show of ecstatic bliss, and his cock literally twitched. This was going to be a long-ass day, one way or another. She kept her eyes closed as she took another caffeine hit. He could not wait to watch her come.

And he was going to watch her come. A lot.

Heat shot through him at the thought. He continued to enjoy his view of her when she opened her eyes and looked up at him.

"Well, you can take me home. I can scrape the guts off my kitchen floor and don a hazmat suit to mop, then maybe I can meet you for dinner? No Italian, though. Me and my close relationship with red sauce are going on a break."

His bark of laughter felt good, and a warm feeling slid through his chest. Hot and funny was a deadly combination. Add to that the fact she was joking about the night before and he felt a blast of admiration for this woman. He liked a lot of people, loved few, and admired few. He was starting to think this woman could have triple-crown potential.

He set the plate with the bagel and the banana on top of the towels he had brought in that morning. He hadn't wanted to invade her privacy any more than necessary, but he would be lying if he said he hadn't taken a second, or thirty, to look at her in bed, asleep and vulnerable. She had looked sweet and young and unconsciously appealing with all that red hair tangled around her head, her lips slightly parted, her face relaxed. A wave of protectiveness followed by ripples of desire had rushed through him then.

Now here she was, being that same effortlessly sweet and funny, but also showing her backbone was hefty. Last night she had weathered one fucked-up shit performance—one that would have shaken the jockstrap on anybody. This morning she was joking about red sauce. He had never known anyone, not in Afghanistan, not in his profession as a nurse, and not in his personal life, who had shown that much bounce back resiliency in such a short amount of time. He realized, as he walked to the big-ass rocking chair he had bought at a flea market a week ago, that it was genuine. He didn't question how he knew something so fundamental after knowing someone less than a month. He just did.

"Love has one eye, uyehi. Look with that eye and trust it. Now make me some pancakes."

He shook his head slightly as he sat down and stretched his legs out in front of him, crossing them at his ankles. Aponi had been a wise person. She had also loved pancakes. She had taught him to trust himself and his feelings about people and situations. He leaned back into the warm wood of the rocking chair and surveyed Olivia Hudson eating a banana.

"I hope you are okay with this, udalii. Because I might be in a bit of trouble here."

His dead wife didn't answer his mental, cosmic email but on this, she didn't have to. He knew how she would be. They had the conversation that all couples had, and they had it early in their relationship, right before he was going to be deployed. Neither of them wanted to leave anything to chance. When one or both of you were going to face a very real possibility of death, shit had to be taken care of.

"It is unbearable for me to think of you alone, Kyle. The only thing worse than not being with you is the thought of you being alone if I'm gone. I literally can't tolerate the fear of that. I swear to God, I'll come back and fix you up."

The amazing part of it was that he had believed her. Getting past his own selfish shit, he actually felt the same. He could see himself being a supernatural wingman all too easily. He'd been alone a lot in his life, if not figuratively then emotionally. He did not have it in him to wish that feeling of isolation and loneliness on anyone, much less someone he loved. But getting here and giving significant thought to letting another woman into his life had been a fucking monumental climb up a dark-ass mountain.

Had been? Did that mean it was over?

"Anybody ever tell you that you look great eating a banana?" He needed to get out of his head for a while.

There was shit to do. Therefore, he went to his go-to, off-color bullshitting. He watched her toss the peel onto the plate and regard him silently, as if weighing options on how to respond. When she answered, he knew he was totally fucked.

"Can we make a pact not to use food metaphors today? I'm still working through my issues with marinara sauce and tube pasta, and I can't address butchering psychos and blow jobs in the same morning."

Yep. Triple-crown potential.

Olivia

She watched him bellow out a laugh that woke Snape and shook the cheap blinds on the bare, rental house windows. God, he was hot when he laughed. She could see herself doing all manner of things to get that laugh. The thought sobered her. That was not such a good thing. Thoughts like that led to potentially bad places for her. It was one thing to contemplate sleeping with him, and she had only toed the waters of that concept during their date. It was a whole different bowl of soup, letting softer emotions in. Wanting to give him an orgasm was one thing. Longing to make him laugh was trouble with a capital T.

She couldn't ignore it. Last night's date was fun, and she wanted another. She had even been good with making out on her couch. Once all hell had broken loose, Kyle had gone from new guy on a first date to a man who took quiet charge, who protected and deflected as much awfulness as he could. Now that she had the ability to reflect, all the small things he had done for her last night came floating back in images that were good pictures to have. This man, with the tattoos and the NSFW vocabulary, was a closet nurturer and caregiver. He was an alpha male grandmother. He'd probably go hunt a wild boar down, wrestle it naked; then carry it on his back through the snow to the cave. Then he'd make you some soup with the meat and rub your feet while you ate it.

In other words, he was perfect for her. She might have to reassess her judgment if he ever showed up at her house in khaki pants, but she figured the chances of that were slim to nonexistent. He was obviously highly intelligent, but he was also street smart. Listening to him discuss theories with Sam last night, she realized now he had not sounded out of his element talking with a law enforcement officer of Sam's caliber.

Sam Beckett was Kyle's best friend since childhood, but he was also a decorated military hero and a former FBI special agent. Last night they had conversed as equals. Laura and Jake had spoken of Kyle's skill as a nurse often over the years. She also knew some of his backstory of no father and a runaway mother, because she lived where she lived. She had witnessed firsthand a bit of his juvenile delinquent period. The man he was, the man he had made himself into, was a sight to behold, and not just physically.

But that body and those eyes and that talented mouth, those were icing on a very appealing cake. He was a man who had found a deep love once, and then lost it. Notwithstanding the fact he was capable of that kind of love and commitment, which was a large part of what made him so appealing, it was also a huge chunk of the problem. She could not ignore the selfish but real part of her that longed to be someone's one and only. She would never be Kyle Valentine's one and only, and that hurt, the ache deep in her belly. Yet, how much of that narrow thinking was an emotional limitation that she built in her own head? Was it possible those romance novel guidelines were just that—fiction—and shallow fiction, at that?

She had read a poem somewhere that said grief was love with no place to go. She had certainly felt the impact of that when she lost her mother, and then her father. There were days and events she longed to share with someone, holidays and good times and failures and losses. She felt she had been damming it all up for so long. Yes, it felt like a dam that was about to burst sometimes.

Love with no place to go.

Did Kyle feel that? Was love, no matter who it was first directed to, always love? Did it need a place to flow, spaces to fill up? Had she been believing in a false narrative? Were the physics of devotion and commitment completely different than what she had narrowly defined them as her entire life?

"Not sure what you were just thinking about, sweetheart, but it's all going to be okay."

His voice jerked her out of her thoughts. She watched as he sat upright in his chair, leaned forward, rested his elbows on his knees, and clasped his hands together.

"Now that you are fortified, I'll tell you what I've been up to while you've been lazing in bed. First, I talked to Laura, who basically gave me the 411 on your entire life. Side note, you might want to talk to her about that. Not sure it's a good idea to spill that much to some yahoo who rides a bike and lives in a cheap rental out on a country road in Tennessee. Just sayin'."

She grinned at him, but she felt a bit uncomfortable. He was right. She and Laura needed to have a talk about this particular yahoo. Mostly she needed to assess how someone being in her private life felt. She wasn't used to having anyone there.

He kept talking.

"Your office appointments are rescheduled, so you've got next week to consider whether you want to burn your house down and start over or not." He seemed to pause to gauge her reactions. She didn't make him wait.

"How the hell did you do that?" She was flabbergasted.

He grinned and kept listing his chores without exactly answering her question. "I talked to your padawan, Bryan. Interesting dude and immensely helpful. He's taking care of the office shit. He said to tell you not to worry and asked if I got pictures of the kitchen. He also told me about your find at the mailbox last week. We're gonna talk about him after we talk about Laura."

Olivia was silent. He had talked to Laura, her closest friend. Then he had talked to Bryan, her employee. Who else had he called? Her aunt, Sophie, in Houston?

When he interrupted her pondering with his next bit of information, she kept her silence. Better to just let him finish before she gave him her opinions about the things he had done. She wasn't sure how she was feeling about it all just then.

"I went over and checked the outside of the house and talked to Sam. The animal was not a domestic dog. It was a coyote. He's not sure what that signals, exactly, but he thought you would want to know that the poor critter wasn't someone's Fido, at least. I told him tidbit semantics were marginally helpful, he told me to fuck myself, and he wants to talk to you later this morning, if you are up to it. He'll be here at around eleven, unless you say otherwise."

He paused and she just stared at him. He regarded her for several moments before continuing, his voice even but his eyes on her were intense and assessing.

"He wants to know about the cats in your yard. He wants to know about anyone and anything that you may have been in contact with lately. Specifically, any situation or circumstance that involves a person with several bolts that need tightening."

By the time he finished with that part of his monologue, she wasn't capable of speech. She just sat and stared at him. She had forgotten about the kittens. How had she forgotten about the kittens?

He leaned farther forward toward her. The next was said in a quieter, more serious tone, and it proved to be the final straw that resulted in her undoing.

"There is a disaster restoration service coming from Knoxville Monday morning. Sam says that the crime lab people will be finished with your house by then. Their logo says they'll make your home like whatever befell it never happened, and they can do it in a day. You'll have to stay out of the house for twenty-four hours afterward, because I'm having them clean all the floors, walls, and whatever else in the house. So, it looks like you will be at the Chateau Valentine at least until Wednesday or Thursday."

He stopped talking and sat, looking at her. She felt her chin quiver and the tears leak and run down the sides of her face. There was no stopping them. In everything he had said, all he had done, the fact he had arranged for someone to clean her house, *her father's house*, of what had been done to it, this broke the dam.

"Baby."

He whispered the word, then he was on the bed beside her, holding her while the water gushed over the barriers.

CHAPTER 9: CROTCH ROCKET

Kyle

Well, fuck.

He hadn't meant to make her cry. He just wanted to make her feel safe and to let her know she didn't have to bear the weight of this shit on her own.

He was out of his chair and beside her in a fraction of a second. He had her in his arms in less time than that, pulling her unresisting body onto his lap and pushing her face gently into his chest. The walls were breaking, and he wanted her close when they fell.

He let her cry, holding her against his body as his own chest tightened. Instinctively he sensed this was something she did not do often. He had been a nurse for a long time, and he knew when tears were crocodile and when they were genuine. From the sounds of her sobs, the quaking of her torso, the way her hands were clutching at his shirt, this had been a long time coming. Maybe its pinnacle was the last twelve hours or so, but the roots of this went deeper. The level of this outburst concerned him. When was the last time she had cleared herself out?

When the storm started to ebb, he gently and slowly lowered them back until they were lying on the bed, side by side, her face now in the crook of his neck. Her breathing began to normalize, but for the occasional hiccupping sob that jarred her body. He felt her breath on his neck and throat, warm and slightly uneven. Moving his hand up over her back lightly, he brushed strands of hair away from her cheek.

"Olivia Mae, this is a sad play to use to get me in a bed with you." He trailed his fingers through the hair at the side of her head before moving his hand to gently rub her back. "I usually need some tequila and a Reese's Cup first." He kept his voice teasing and light, but he had an overwhelming urge to get on his bike and go hunting the sick fuck from the night past. He also wanted to know the other perpetrators behind those tears, so he could deal with them too.

"I've got tequila, but it's currently in my serial killer kitchen. I had to improvise." Her voice was muffled against his shoulder.

Reluctantly, he pulled back away from her slightly, enough so he could see her face. Her eyes were a drowned blue and reddened. Her face was wet. He couldn't resist moving his hand and scraping a thumb over one of her cheeks to wipe some of the moisture away.

"It's gonna all be okay, Olivia Mae. You have the word of a Southern gentleman." He whispered this and he did not give a solitary fuck how it sounded. He meant every syllable.

She sniffed and another hiccup escaped. He felt the hand that was clamped on to the side of his shirt relax slightly.

Her voice was shaky when she replied, "I never knew they allowed Southern gentlemen to ride motorcycles. I thought you were all restricted to trusty steeds or four-wheelers."

He chuckled and moved his palm to the back of her head, tightening his arms to hug her gently. He could not help it. She was so damn cute. He made the hug brief, then moved back so he could again meet her eyes.

"So you're good with everything—Bryan and the cleaning company?"

"I'm embarrassed at how willing I am to let you be all alpha-male-take-charge, but yes. I hadn't even let myself think about anything practical yet." He watched her move her eyes to stare at some spot in the vicinity of his ear. "Thank you." The words were whispered, and he sensed them against his skin. They felt nice.

"And you're all right with talking to Sam?" He felt her take a deep breath on this one before answering.

She brought her eyes back to his. "No. But I have to because it has to be done. What I'd really like to do is go for a long ride and not have to think about anything but what might be around the next bend in the road. And maybe get some ice cream." She tried to grin but failed. Fuck. He couldn't get her out of talking to Sam. However, he could take her on a ride when it was over.

He began to comb his fingers through the thick strands of her hair as she relaxed into him and rested her head on his shoulder. He lay with her in his arms, letting her quiet and regain her composure. Damn, this felt so right. If he closed his eyes and let his mind go, he could imagine it was just another Saturday morning with her in his bed, in his arms, talking about what they were going to do that day.

"Are you averse to all vehicles without doors?" He remembered her conditions on going on their non-date.

She snuggled closer, and let go of the side of his shirt, and brought her hand up to rest at his chest. Definitely nice.

"Only on first dates. I actually dated a guy in college who had a bike. It was great fun to take into the mountains."

He did not want to know about any guys she had dated who had bikes. "Yeah? You dated a Harley man in your misbegotten youth, huh?" He felt her give a giggle.

"No, he didn't have a Harley. It was a Honda or Kawasaki or one of those."

He moved his head slightly so he could breathe in the scent of her hair. Clean and fresh. He wondered what she looked like with it wet and tangled in the shower.

He laughed. "Then you did not date a man with a bike. You dated a lad with a crotch rocket and, odds are, a malfunctioning dick of questionable size."

He felt her jerk back away from him and instantly regretted his smart-ass comment.

But she was barely suppressing a smile when she

admonished, "Are you suggesting that a man's vehicle is truly a measure of his, um, talent and attributes?"

He didn't stop himself from taking advantage of the moment. Moving swiftly, he pushed her over onto her back and moved to hover over her, looking down at her and liking very much what he saw.

"I would say the true measure of a man and his attributes has to do with how he deals with an opportune moment such as this one." He lowered his head, pausing just before he took her mouth, a thing he had been waiting to do for way too long. "I'm gonna kiss you, Olivia Mae. Then I'll take you for a ride in the hills, and it won't be on a crotch rocket. When we get back, I'll introduce you formally to Beast, we'll deal with Sam, then I'll feed you real food." He moved his head until his mouth was less than a millimeter from hers. "Later on, we can watch a movie and maybe feel each other up. You good with all that?"

He didn't wait for an answer.

Olivia

When his tongue slipped into her mouth, a flood of warmth hit her lower belly. It wasn't subtle and it wasn't a hint. It might have been the remnants of her emotion overload, but she didn't think so. It was him. The attraction she was experiencing was physical, emotional, intellectual, and very personal. They might have technically only been on one date, but they had just spent some intense hours together. While she was uncomfortable with all of her he had seen, she was dazed by all of him she had experienced.

You couldn't fake how you dealt with crises, whether

you were the victim or the bystanders or the cavalry sent in to clean up. Kyle had shown himself to be cool, considerate, caring, and protective. Here in his house, he was funny and sweet, not to mention sexy. The timing might be questionable, but she did not care just then. So she moved her hands up to pull his head down closer and kissed him back.

When she pushed to get him closer, he slipped an arm around her waist and pulled her up, crushing their bodies together from chest to thighs. He tilted his head and coaxed her lips open wider, giving himself better access. She was so absolutely good with that and offered her mouth to him eagerly. He curled his tongue around hers, sliding his wetly and skillfully, and the feeling was the most intensely erotic thing she had ever felt in her life.

Olivia was not a virgin. She'd had sex. She'd had what she would consider good sex. She had never in her life had a kiss like this one. Digging her nails into his scalp, she moaned into his mouth. She felt one of his legs move to push gently, making room for itself between hers as she moved to accommodate him. His hand left her back to thread his fingers into the hair at her nape, his hand tightening there as the kiss got harder, wetter, and more delicious. He tugged her hair at the same time he bit into her lower lip, and Olivia's pelvis pushed against the hard muscle of his thigh. He released her mouth, but only to bend his head and scrape his teeth lightly down the skin below her left ear. The touch sent a shiver through her body.

"Jesus, you taste good." This was hissed through his

teeth as his breath came unevenly at her ear. "I can't wait to taste your nipples." He nipped the skin behind her ear. "And your pussy." He dug his teeth into the skin of her earlobe hard enough to almost be painful. Olivia felt the muscles between her legs quake.

Dear God, she wanted him to do that, like immediately.

"Kyle..." She didn't get to say anything else. He moved his leg from between hers and pushed back a few inches. He looked into her face and his eyes were heavy with arousal. What he saw on her face he seemed to like, because a look of satisfaction came over his features before he spoke.

"Baby, we need to get off this bed. I am a Harley man, but I ain't Superman, and if I have that mouth one more time, Sam is gonna have to wait until tomorrow, or possibly next month. So get your fine ass up, take a shower, dally with whatever doodads that need dallied with. Mr. Police Chief Man will be here in less than an hour."

With that he bent his head and placed a loud, smacking kiss on her lips. Then he heaved himself off the bed. He clicked his tongue to Snape, and man and dog left the room without looking back. It was for the best because she needed to get her act together. She felt like she had just been left in mid-ravage. Her lips were heated with the blood pulsing in them, her legs were trembling, and her sex felt hot and achy.

Holy shit, the man was something else. She had to get a shower and put some semblance of reality back into her brain. Pushing up off the bed, she reached for the stack of towels and then looked around for her overnight bag. By the time she left the bathroom that was across the hall from the bedroom, showered, dressed, and "doodadded," as it were, she felt nearly normal.

Ninety minutes later, she didn't feel quite so normal. She felt pissed off, scared shitless, and loaded for bear. Because within those ninety minutes she learned who had slaughtered a coyote in her kitchen, why they had done it, and that she couldn't do a damn thing about it.

CHAPTER 10: CRAZY SOUTHERN PEOPLE

Olivia

Kyle exploded out of his seat.

"What the fuck do you mean, you can't arrest her? You've got the goddamn camera footage!"

Olivia sat silent and stunned. She turned her attention to Sam Beckett, who was presently sitting in a green plastic lawn chair in Kyle's only partially furnished living room. He had been sitting there for a half hour, the beer Kyle had gotten him untouched on the folding TV table beside the chair.

After her shower she had ventured out into the living area of the house. The smell of fresh paint and wood floor refinishing was a bit stronger, and the obvious evidence of a recent remodel was everywhere, from the blue plastic film that still covered the dishwasher door to the green painter's tape that someone had forgotten to peel off the side of the front door casing.

There was a couch covered in charcoal gray fabric in the middle of the living area floor. It did not look worn, but it did look comfortable. Next to it was the green plastic lawn chair. The TV table had a twin on the far side of the couch. It held a ginger jar lamp like the one in the bedroom, navy this time, with two television remotes. There was no coffee table. Against the wall facing the couch was an entertainment unit that held a ridiculously large television and little else. Some distance behind the couch, and closer to the open kitchen, was a gorgeous dining table. It was round, with a fat pedestal, and its deep walnut wood gleamed in the sunlight that was streaming through more unadorned windows. On either side of it were two more green plastic lawn chairs. Olivia thought it was a travesty to have those chairs at that magnificent table.

The kitchen was on the other side of the open floor plan. It was clean and functional, with white cabinets, a black-and-white tile floor, and a basic double stainless-steel sink. There was a coffee maker and a toaster on the expanse of laminate counter.

Kyle had been at the fridge when she walked out. He shut the door to the refrigerator and moved to lean back against the counter beside it, crossing his arms over the tight, purple, long-sleeved Prince tee shirt he had on. Now how had she missed that shirt? But she knew. She was too busy admiring the expanse of chest it covered.

She grinned at him. "Prince? Somehow I thought you would be a Lenny Kravitz man." She stopped at the side of the dining table. She couldn't resist reaching out to touch the wood and see if it was as smooth as it looked. "This table is beautiful. Where did you get it?"

"Aponi and I found it and fixed it up." His words made her hand still on the tabletop. Her first instinct was to apologize. She stopped herself. She should not assume it was unpleasant for him to have that memory triggered. His voice had been matter-of-fact. She asked a question and he answered. She moved her hand across the surface again, before turning into the living room. She surveyed the living area and turned to him with a wider grin.

"Did you consult Bachelors R Us for your décor?"

He pushed away from the counter and walked slowly toward her. Instantly her mouth got dry. Who was that sexy just walking across a room, for heaven's sake? She did not need him to get close enough to touch her right then. It was just too much. Therefore, she moved away from him to the far side of the couch. He stopped walking and stood watching her, his arms again crossed on his chest. His expression looked like he was weighing the risks and benefits before he answered.

"Nope. I purchased the finest Ikea has to offer. Spared no expense. I even ate two orders of meatballs while I was there trying to learn Swedish." He made the joke, but he didn't smile. She would know why when he continued.

"We are going to need to talk about quite a list of things, I see." She watched his face gentle and his voice got softer.

"There's that sweater you wore last night, and the fact you need to learn what a door lock is for. I need to express to you the importance of having Reese's Cups readily available for your man, and..." he paused and his look intensified, "...we need to address the fact I was married to a woman I loved, and she died."

Her man? "Kyle..."

He held up a hand. "No, sweetheart. I get to say this real quick. We will talk about it later, and everything will be okay. But I gotta get this out now."

He took the three steps it required for him to be standing directly in front of her. He put his big, warm hands on her shoulders and at his touch she swallowed. Then he bent his head down slightly to make allowances for their disparity in height. His expression was serious, and his demeanor was demanding, compelling her to look into his eyes. She swallowed hard again as she stared up into his face.

"Yes, that table belonged to me and my dead wife. It is a fantastic fucking memory for me to have. I keep it because of that, because it's beautiful, and it represents something that is special to me. That table is a lot of things but it is not is a sign of me being stuck in some kind of grief quicksand, and I don't want you to think that every damn time you walk by it. Do you get what I'm saying? That table is as much a part of my life as the marlin I caught and mounted that will get hung up in this room. It is as much a part of me as the tattoo of a leprechaun I got on my leg when I was fifteen and stupid."

He paused for a moment, and brought his hands up to cup her face, drawing her forward, and tilting her jaw so his eyes were all she could see.

"When you get me a birthday present or a Christmas present, it will become a part of me, a special part, because it will come from you. It will become a part of my life that I will never get rid of or apologize for having. And if what is happening between us goes south, I'll still keep it, because it will still represent a fucking good memory."

He finished bending his head to her and gently kissed her lips. "Got it?" This was whispered so close the breath from it caressed her cheek.

Olivia brought her hands up to hold his forearms in their grasp. She squeezed lightly and answered him. When she did, the words and the insight behind them were spontaneous, but they were real and true. As she spoke, she felt the weight of something bad suddenly leave her spirit. Because she got it. She got it and it felt wonderful to have that load disappear.

"I keep my house with six bedrooms and a ridiculous electricity bill because it was my father's house." The next made her smile gently at him.

"I have a blanket that my mother crocheted while she was pregnant with me." She tightened her fingers on him farther. "I still have the movie ticket stubs from the first date I had with the guy who I had sex for the first time with, even though he turned out to be unable to grasp the concept of exclusivity." She stood on tiptoe and brushed her lips against his cheek. "I get it." She flattened her feet back to the floor and grinned up at him. "I am going to need to see that leprechaun, however, before I fully commit."

He threw back his head and laughed, wrapping his arms around her and pulling her in for a bear hug. "Olivia Mae, you are something else."

A knock sounded at the door and the conversation was over. She had to go talk about a psycho in her house with a cop, but standing there in Kyle Valentine's arms, held against his big body, was the safest and happiest she had ever felt in her life.

Kyle

He could not fucking wrap his head around what Sam had just told them.

There was a video of the woman, carrying a load of dead coyote over her shoulder, walking over the bridge from the church parking lot to Olivia's backyard. The almost three-minute video showed the bitch carrying her shit up the back steps and going *into Olivia's fucking house*. The custodian of the church gave his phone with the recording to the officer who did the canvas of the neighborhood at six that morning. Who the fuck knew why the guy hadn't called the cops when he was filming.

Olivia had said what he was thinking at that point.

"So did you arrest her? What happens now?"

When Sam answered her, two and two started to make seventeen, and Kyle felt like he wanted to ram his fist through his brand-new sixty-inch television with the NASA-designed remote.

Sam had sat forward in his seat and clasped his hands together. Kyle knew that positioning all too well, and he started to feel a trickle of dread. Papa Sam was about to impart all the reasons why you weren't going to get what you wanted, and Kyle knew he was most certainly not going to like what he heard.

"Charlotte Winston Barksdale has a very impressive gaggle of psychiatrists and a crumbling plantation load of money. She also has a butt load of very established Tennessee lawyers. They contacted me this morning, bright and early, right after my squad car of officers attempted to question Ms. Winston Barksdale at said crumbling mansion."

Kyle turned his attention to Olivia and watched as the color drained from her pretty face.

"Charlie Barksdale? Charlie Barksdale is who broke into my house?" Her voice was full of disbelief.

"Yeah," Sam replied. "Cooter Johnson filmed it with his phone, but he recognized her and her Mercedes. She's not exactly an incognito type around town."

Anyone with a passing connection to Faithful knew who Charlie Barksdale was. She was the last of the Barksdale family, the reclusive middle-aged spinster who was all that was left of a once powerful family. The Barksdale money had been made on the backs of slavery pre-Civil War, and had continued unabated during Reconstruction, thanks to sharecropping, marrying up, and the fact that they had owned over fifteen hundred acres of prime Tennessee farmland.

Charlotte Winston Barksdale's grandfather had made millions more in the stock market. His son, Abbott "Abby" Winston Barksdale III, who had a not-insignificant psychiatric history, had pulled it all out of the markets. He holed it up in the Faithful Municipal Bank, of which there was exactly one branch, and in various cigar boxes scattered around the mansion. He barely touched enough of it to maintain the eight thousand square foot antebellum monstrosity that comprised the family dwelling. His wife had run off to places unknown, leaving their six-year-old daughter and the money behind.

When Charlie Barksdale buried Old Man Barksdale, he was eighty-seven, she was fifty-one, and she had never left the big house for more than a day or two since she came home from The Webb Boarding School at eighteen. Once Abby Barksdale was buried in the family plot, Charlie promptly sold all but the ten acres the main house and old slave quarters stood on to a developer from Nashville. For the last few years, she had set about filling up the nineteen-room edifice with as many cats, dogs, pygmy goats, and birds as she could accumulate.

That's when Olivia had gotten to know her.

"Livie, I need to know exactly how you became involved with Charlotte Barksdale. I got the story secondhand from Rhonda and I remember the bones of the case, but I want to hear it all from you. Maybe you have some information I can use." Sam was casting a lure out to get a bite, any way he could. Kyle was at least feeling good about that.

He watched as Olivia frowned, then answered.

"Well, my father used to go up and take care of her animals. She would call him, tell him what was going on, he would get whatever he thought he would need, and go out and take care of it. In a day or two, there would be an envelope in the mailbox with just his name on it. No stamp or anything. It would have money in it—cash. Sometimes he would say it was too much, put back in the envelope what he decided she had overpaid, and take it back out to her. I never really had any contact with her until after he died."

Kyle watched and saw the shadow pass over her face. Something else they needed to talk about.

She continued, "About, maybe a year after he passed, I got a call from her. She said one of her dogs was sick and she needed me to come out. I tried asking her questions, I remember, but she just insisted that I come out. So I packed a bag and went." Olivia closed her eyes and took a couple of breaths.

"When I got out there, what I saw was the worst case of animal hoarding I've ever witnessed. I saw some sights when I was in vet school, but this was unbelievable. There were animals and birds all over the house, young ones, old ones, sick ones. The sight was horrific and the smell even worse. Charlie led me through the downstairs like she didn't even see what was around her."

Kyle watched Olivia grimace at the memory, and her voice was hoarse when she kept talking. "I had to put down the dog on the spot. It was a beagle puppy." She cleared her throat and looked at Sam. "I drove off the property, parked on the side of the road, and called your people and the Knoxville ASPCA. We spent four days getting the animals out of the house. They placed the ones that didn't have to be euthanized."

More shadows crossed her face as those memories crawled out. "I had to have help from Knoxville to handle all the dogs and cats. The large animal vet from Maryville took the goats and the avian vet school from UT took all the birds. TV people from Knoxville and Nashville were parked in my parking lot for a couple of weeks."

She grimaced and the sarcasm was evident in her voice. "Not every day a rich old Southern lady gets arrested and then confined to a state institution because she had goats sleeping in bed with her." She looked at him and then back to Sam. "I gave a statement but that was the last of it, as far as I was concerned. She was back at the mansion within a month and, other than seeing her occasionally in the Food Lion, that's it. I haven't spoken to her since. The police didn't follow up with me, and the news reported that she had gone through treatment and was prohibited from owning animals for a year."

They were all silent for several minutes. Finally, Sam spoke.

"Apparently, she has been pretty unhappy with you, I would say. But money, lawyers, and privileged information are making it so that my office doesn't have a lot of options. I spoke to the circuit judge myself this morning, and the DA. The judge denied a search warrant of the mansion. The DA, who went to Vanderbilt with her chief counsel, says there's not enough evidence to justify bringing her in for questioning, and Cooter Johnson is not exactly a star witness, since he's in the drunk tank at the station more than he's at home in his trailer."

He raked his hand through his short, sandy hair and Kyle knew it was in massive frustration. Sam Beckett did not like being thwarted by bullshit and cronyism.

"Look, I watched the video from the phone. I can't identify her, and Cooter failed to get a shot of her plate." Sam stood. "I would suggest strongly that you get a good security system put in your house, get some pepper spray and/or a stun gun, and let Prince here hang with you until I can sort this out a little bit more."

He moved his attention to Kyle. "And you should take her down to the gym and give her the benefit of all that time and money you spent learning how to kill people with your left elbow."

Olivia stood as well, and Kyle watched Sam as his expression turned from the cop to the friend. When he spoke to Olivia, his voice was gentle.

"Olivia, I'm going to have a car drive by every night. I wish I could do more. I'm serious about the security system. I can give you some names of reputable companies that will come out and install in less than a week. In the meantime, as much as it pains me to say it, I think you should keep Prince here around. He's got nothing better to do, and the face scares away pretty much everybody." He smiled at her.

Kyle moved to stand beside Olivia. He put an arm around her shoulders and was gratified when she moved closer to him. Then he addressed Sam. In earlier times, he would have flipped the other man off and told him how and why to go fuck himself. He didn't do any of this. He was dead serious when he spoke.

"She's not going to be alone."

CHAPTER 11: BIKE RIDE

Olivia

"Get your coat."

Olivia was standing in the same spot she had been in when Sam had given his last bit of advice, and he had been gone a full ten minutes. She was staring sightlessly at the door.

Charlie Barksdale, who was admittedly a kook by anyone's measure but everyone in town considered to be just another harmless eccentric, was not your everyday Southern front porch lunatic. She had somehow gotten a coyote, killed it, carried it up and into Olivia's house, and filleted it on the kitchen counter. She had done this for God only knew what reason, but the prevailing law enforcement theory was she was extremely pissed off at Olivia for taking her ability to have seventeen goats away.

She shivered at the picture in her mind of the entrails of the animal hanging over the lip of her butcher-block countertop. Butcher-block. Jesus, that was almost funny, in a Stephen King novel kind of way. She startled when Kyle spoke to her from the other side of the room.

"Baby, get your coat. We're going for that ride."

She looked at him, saying nothing. He looked back and raised his eyebrows, a ghost of a manufactured grin on his face.

"Olivia Mae, I cannot educate you about real men with bikes unless you go get your coat."

The question she asked had nothing to do with the current crazy circling around her.

"Why do you call me that? My middle name is Frances." She never told anyone her middle name. She was pretty sure she had just given him way more ammunition with which to tease her than was wise.

"Frances, huh? Not as bad as some, I guess." She felt a bit of relief. She really disliked her middle name. Better to let it go and not show weakness.

"What's yours?"

He shook his head. "Oh no. That will not be happening in broad daylight."

Now what did that mean?

He yanked the black leather jacket she had drooled over off a hook by the front door. Pulling it on, he kept talking. "You know who Brett Young is?"

She didn't ask the obvious about what the question had to do with anything. "Yes. Country singer from, of all places, California. Cute, tall, played baseball, I think I heard somewhere." Then it dawned on her. "Oh yeah, the song, "Olivia Mae." Favorite of yours, Mr. Paisley Park?" She gestured toward the tee shirt.

He walked to her and took her arm at her elbow,

guiding her out of the living area and down the short hall to the bedrooms.

"How about we get your coat? I'll introduce you to Beast, then we'll get on my bike. Music is a subject that cannot be rushed. Besides, our future relationship will be determined by that conversation, and I need to see your fine ass on the bike before we part ways over you liking Nickelback or some shit."

She got her coat, briefly met Beast, who apparently had tremendous attitude about dogs and was therefore sulking in Kyle's bedroom. The big gray Russian blue had gorgeous golden eyes and was completely aware of how stunningly beautiful he was. He allowed Olivia to briefly stroke his head then sauntered away from her to return to his throne by the window. He gave not the first acknowledgment to Kyle that he even recognized the man's existence. She observed that Kyle didn't seem to care in the least.

"See ya later, asshole." He closed the bedroom door on the cat.

Olivia then let Snape out into the small fenced-in backyard for a brief potty break and five-minute run, which was all he required. She squatted in front of the big dog and jabbered nonsensically to him, while Kyle disappeared to somewhere and came back carrying a black motorcycle helmet with a smoked visor and a tag still hanging from the strap.

She straightened from the big dog, who promptly lumbered over to the small area rug in front of the couch, stretched out with a groan, and was asleep almost immediately.

"You have a dysfunctional relationship with your cat."

She took the helmet from his outstretched hands and examined it, trying it on and finding that it fit. He moved to stand in front of her and took the straps from her, fiddling with the clasps until he was satisfied with the adjustment. He handed her the small crossbody bag she had thrown on the couch and she slipped it over her the helmet, tweaking the strap of it across her chest and shoulder.

"You have a codependent relationship with your dog." He grinned. "One man's dysfunction is another man's amicable rapport."

She moved to follow him to the door, admiring the snug fit of his jeans over his behind. "Yeah, well, call me about my codependency when you have Dexter's crazy aunt remodeling your kitchen."

He turned abruptly at the door, a blinding smile on his lips. "You know who Brett Young *and* Dexter are. Fuck me, Olivia Mae, but if you like AC/DC and being on top, you may be the perfect woman." He bent and planted another of his loud, smacking kisses on her speechless lips.

Well hell, how was she supposed to respond to that?

She was on the Harley before she remembered how she should be scared and worried about all the crap going on in her life. Instead she was picturing herself riding him in that big-ass rocking chair, his tongue in her mouth, and his big hands holding her in place.

More than that, she was thinking how much she liked him calling her the perfect woman.

Kyle

He pulled the Harley Fat Boy leisurely into the rest area and observation point. They were about halfway through the Cherahala Skyway drive, and he wanted to take a break and check Olivia's mental temperature. He also wanted to spend some time taking in the beauty of his home state. He hadn't made this trek since he had left Faithful, and the last time through had not been a time he relished recalling. It was the day before he left for Florida, and it had been a goodbye trip. At the time, he hadn't considered that he would ever come back.

He cut the engine and flipped the stand. He waited for her to dismount and missed the heat of her when she was standing by the rear tire and not plastered to him any longer. Damn, but she felt good back there; the insides of her thighs pressed to the outsides of his, her arms around his waist. The thought made him feel like shit, but he couldn't help but remember the fact that Aponi had not liked motorcycles. She hadn't given him shit about it, but neither could she be persuaded to ride with him often.

He wondered how he would feel if he and Olivia's positions were reversed. If it was she who had been in love with someone so deeply she had married them and mourned them for years after they were gone. With another damning self-realization, he knew it would have been hard as fuck for him to deal with. Damn, but dealing with all this history and baggage was for shit. He sat on the bike as she removed her helmet, shook out her hair, and looked around.

"Nothing good is easy, Kyle. Nothing. You can do easy and

have shit for a life. Or you can get your head out of your ass and have better."

His juvenile probation officer had told him that when he was seventeen and had gotten himself picked up, again, by the cops for any one of a dozen reasons he could no longer remember. At the time he probably had told the guy to go fuck himself and his advice. But it was one of the few things people had tried to tell him that had stuck. Then he met Aponi and she made it make sense.

If he was going to have what he wanted with Olivia, he needed to man the fuck up. He also had to be mindful of how she felt. Her reaction to the table and what she had shared made him feel hopeful that she was up to the challenge. He didn't want to be something else she had to work to deal with, but he was thirty-nine years old and not fresh out of the wrapper. Thinking back on the shadows that always crossed her face when she mentioned her father, he knew she had shit too. He needed to find out what that shit was. Then maybe they could deal with their collective shit and have a damn second date.

Of course, technically, they were still on their first date. He grinned inwardly. If he had his way and she was on board, they were going to fuck on their first date. He swung his leg over the Harley. First, he wanted to look at the mountains with her.

Three hours later, he pulled the Fat Boy into the garage of the rental. They had a kick-ass day, all things considered. They had completed the Skyway run, eaten some good barbecue at a hole-in-the-wall, and laughed a lot. He had also learned quite a bit about her. He learned about vet school and how she had broken her arm delivering a baby llama. He found out she didn't like to fly, and her favorite movie was *As Good As It Gets*. He told her some about the people of Afghanistan and a couple of his favorite nursing war stories. They nearly came to blows about music.

She got in his face about Janis Joplin and Ann Wilson and Lady Gaga. He got in hers about Slash and Eric Clapton and Eddie Van Halen. They agreed that Jason Isbell was a songwriting master, and that *Die Hard* was a Christmas movie. He was disappointed she knew next to nothing about Motown, but her eyes and her ass balanced that failing.

And she opened up about her father. It was when they were sitting on the open-air porch of the barbecue place, their bellies full and the sun setting. He asked the question while they were close, their hips touching on the bench. He had his arm around her and was fiddling with the end of the braid she had woven into her hair. She was relaxed, her feet up on the porch rail in front of them.

"Were you and your dad close?"

He didn't feel her reaction, but the atmosphere of relaxation evaporated. He didn't like that, but he wasn't surprised. He waited, wondering if she was going to tell him it was none of his business. She didn't. Instead, she took a deep breath and blew it out, like she was getting ready to deal with something really unpleasant. When she spoke, he knew that was exactly what it was to her. He observed as she seemed to consciously make herself relax. She kept her eyes on the mountains in front of her when she finally answered him.

"No." He watched as she closed her eyes for a moment, before opening them and continuing. "My mother died when I was young, and I blamed him, even though she died of cancer and he had nothing to do with it." She dropped her attention to her hand, which had begun to pick with great concentration at a thread poking out of her jeans. "I was grieving and angry and didn't know how to handle the loss. Then I hit puberty and became a really spoiled little bitch."

He moved his hand to clasp the nape of her neck. "Hey, look, you don't have to answer this now." Shit. He should have waited. He had assumed, from the air of sadness that had shown across her face whenever her father was mentioned, they had a good relationship, that the sadness was plain and simple sadness over the death of her father.

She turned her face to him and smiled a brief, heartbreaking smile before facing the mountains once again.

"No, it's good. I've just never talked about this honestly with anyone. It makes people uncomfortable. And I know you get it that people do not want to bring up loss to you, even if you need them to." She placed her hand lightly on his thigh, and he felt that thing in his chest that felt at once painful and good.

"My father met a woman when I was thirteen. She

was a schoolteacher. I'm not sure how he met her, because I couldn't be bothered to have him share with me. He tried to get us to know each other, and in retrospect she was a perfectly lovely woman, from what I can remember now. But she wasn't my mother, and I didn't give a damn about anything but what I wanted."

She paused, and he heard the break in her voice when she continued, "So I made it impossible for him to have her."

She cleared her throat and moved her hand away from him, returning to the task of picking at her jeans. "After that we just drifted farther and farther apart. I came back to take over the practice because it was what I always wanted, but our relationship never healed. He wasn't cruel or confrontational or anything. He simply worked, ate his meals, watched television in his den, and died before I woke up and apologized for forcing him to live alone."

He saw a drop of moisture fall to soak the fabric of her jeans near where the white thread pushed through the blue denim.

He gently squeezed her neck. "Baby, you know that he was a grown man, and you were a child, right? I mean, nothing but love, but he had all the power and the means to deal with a kid. He was an educated man, I assume. He could have taken steps to help you cope, deal with your loss." He moved his hand to encircle her with his arm and pull her closer to him on the seat. "Yeah, you might have been a little shit. But you were also a kid, who did not have the tools to see things with any perspective."

He turned a pressed a brief kiss to the top of her head and that thing in his chest expanded when she let her head rest on his shoulder. "Listen, I am not the grief fairy, but I do know a thing or two about guilt. It's a useless emotion. It's past shit and it is just that—in the past. All it does is keep you from living now." He kissed the top of her head again and tightened his arm around her.

"Aponi told me something once that her grandfather told her. It's basically this. There are two wolves fighting in everyone's soul. One is regret and self-pity and guilt and a bunch of other negative shit. The other one is serenity and grace and hope, and all the shit that makes us worthy of higher thinking. The wolf who will win the fight is the one you feed."

He brought her completely into the circle of his arms and held her against his chest. She was silent but she moved into his embrace fully. "I spent three years feeding the wrong fucker, Olivia. I was pretty sure at the time I knew who was going to win, and I was fine with it. But the people who love us are not fine with us living what short time we have wasting our existence on grief, guilt, and regret."

He shut up because it occurred to him how much sense what he had just said made, and how little of it was from him. It was from his probation officer and from Aponi, Aunt Rhonda, Sam, Aunt Grace, his cousin, John, and his CO in basic training. It was from every person who had seen something in him worth saving, and, when he was at his lowest, had stepped in to pull him up when he couldn't pull himself.

Olivia turned her face into his neck and snaked her arm firmly across his stomach, and his chest felt like it might explode with the goodness of it.

"Did anybody ever tell you how smart you are for a guy who thinks Slash is a better guitar player than Eddie Van Halen?"

He smiled even though she couldn't see him. "Thank you, Frances."

CHAPTER 12: FISH OR CUT BAIT

Olivia

Somewhere between the barbecue joint and pulling into the garage, Olivia had decided she was going to sleep with Kyle Valentine, and she was going to do it that night.

The catalyst could have been the two panty-melting kisses, or the Harley, or the fact he called his cat an asshole, or his holding her while she talked about her father. It was probably a combination of all that, the tattoos, the leather jacket, and the fact he was the sexiest man she had ever seen. Whatever potluck stew of sexual attraction ingredients it was, it was going to happen.

When the motor died in the garage of his house, she didn't get off the Harley. She reached up and hurriedly unsnapped the helmet and pulled it off, setting it on the floor next to the bike. She fit the front of her body once more into the back of his and moved her hands back into place at his stomach, just as though they were still riding. He didn't move to dismount. She felt his body still when her hand slid over his stomach. He wasn't tense, exactly, but his body didn't twitch a muscle. He seemed to be waiting for her.

The helmet he wore was what she heard termed a "brain bucket" when she was in college. It was a black half helmet with no visor. She hadn't asked, not wanting to offend, but she considered it was useless as a safety device. It did, however, serve to make his biker hotness level increase by about twenty percent. It also made it easy to talk to him. She moved to put her face close to his exposed ear and said what she wanted to say before she lost her nerve.

"Thank you for today."

He remained silent, the fingers of his hands still wrapped around the grips.

She went on. "Thank you for calling Bryan and bringing me water and a bagel and the towels. Thank you for listening about my father."

"Sweetheart..." She didn't let him finish demurring.

"Most of all thank you for wearing these jeans. I really, really want to see you take them off."

Then she did something she had never done in her life. She moved one of her hands to palm his crotch. Cold call, no heat of the moment, nothing. She wanted to touch him, so she did just that. The muscles of his entire body hardened, and she felt and heard his indrawn hiss of breath.

Then she was getting off the bike because he had twisted at the waist, took her arm, and was pulling her off. His hands were on her and she was up and straddling his lap where he sat on the bike before she could breathe or speak. He growled low in his throat.

"Fucking hell." His mouth took hers, his tongue thrusting, his teeth pulling at her bottom lip. His hands cupped her behind and yanked her crotch tight to his. He pulled harder and her sex was flush against him. She could feel the hardness of him there, behind the fabric of his jeans. She pushed her pelvis forward, sucked his tongue hard, and he groaned so deep she felt it between her legs. The garage was cold. It was winter. But the combustion of heat between their bodies was off the charts. Never had she gotten so aroused so fast. She had been planning this since they were on the road home. Visions of him naked, of them in bed, were quickly replaced with a desire to have him inside her right there on his Harley.

She wanted her coat off. She wanted his jacket off. She wanted their skin to be against each other. She cried out against his mouth when he lifted her up until the heat at the juncture of her thighs was rubbing against his stomach. Gasping his name, she threw her head back in pleasure, as he held her with one hand and arm, using the other hand to push up her sweater and jerk down the cup of her bra. Cold air hit her skin and he clamped his mouth around her nipple and sucked hard, making her nearly scream with the pleasure of it.

Too soon his mouth was back on hers, drinking and tasting. She clasped his head in both her hands and tried to take her fill of him. It was impossible. She couldn't get enough of his taste and his smell. The silence in the garage was broken by their breathing and the sounds of their mouths feasting on each other.

He ended the frenzy by setting her body back down on his lap and slowing the strokes of his tongue against hers. She followed his lead, shaken at how fast they had hit the edge of control. Kyle separated their mouths and pulled her hard into his arms, pushing her face into the crook of his neck. She struggled for oxygen as her heart pounded so loud, she was sure he could hear it. His breathing was uneven, and she marveled that he might feel a fraction of her arousal.

The timbre of his voice, harsh with need, told its own story. "Jesus, fuck, Olivia. Jesus." He dragged in a deep breath and she felt his chest expand with. "Baby, we gotta get a grip for a minute. It's colder than a well digger's ass out here, and as much as I want my dick inside you, we are gonna have to do the bike thing when it gets warmer."

He moved her back, but only so he could kiss her again. This kiss was less heated, softer, his tongue just playing with the tip of hers. He broke it and slid his mouth to the skin of her neck, and then to her ear. Her hands fisted the fabric at the front of his shirt. Olivia had to force herself not to wrap her legs around his waist and put a lot of effort into changing his mind about vehicular sex in the wintertime.

His mouth was hot on her skin as he muttered, "Baby, I've got an inventory of things I want to do to you right now, and one of them is not freezing my dick off in this garage. We're going inside and my firm intention is to feel you up against my front door."

He slid his tongue around the shell of her ear and kept talking. "I want my fingers deep in your pussy. I want to feel that silk and that tight. I want to feel you get wet for me. Then I'm going to eat you on my new Ikea couch."

She felt heat flood her belly and the muscles in the walls of her vagina contracted like he was already there. He didn't stop talking, but he did pause long enough to suck her earlobe into his mouth and bite down gently.

"Then I'm going to kick Beast's ass out and we're going to fuck in my bed, and, baby, you should prepare, because my headboard is solid wood, and the neighbors are close." He brought his mouth back to hers and kissed her again. It was open-mouthed and slow, and Olivia felt an exquisite ache between her legs, her toes curling in her boots.

He ended the kiss and put his hands to the sides of her head, pulling back to look into her eyes. "Are we on the same page here, Olivia Mae?"

That was it. He wanted to make sure it was all good with her. She didn't even consider making him wait when she whispered, "Same book, same page, same paragraph."

Kyle

He had been serious when he listed all the ways he wanted to make her come. He just got the logistics a little fucked.

Because they didn't stop at the door. When she took her jacket off and he paused to fully admire her tits in that fucking red sweater, he went off the rails a bit. He had tried not to ogle all damn day, but he was done with that shit. He'd gotten a glimpse and a taste of what was under that sweater and he was done speculating about her breasts. He ripped off his jacket and threw it in the direction of the wall where the coat hooks were. He reached out a hand and grabbed her jacket, pulling her toward him with it.

She came to him, her eyes dark in the shadows of the light that burned over the stove in the kitchen area and the muted moonlight that shone through the windows. She didn't stumble and she didn't pull back. She kept her eyes locked with his as she took the few steps forward until she was standing so close to him, he could hear her breathing. She spoke and it made him slow his roll. His dick was ready for kick-off, no doubt. It was her sweet, husky voice that made his higher instincts get things calmed down for a minute.

"I'd like to amend our game plan, if that's okay." The words were said low, her voice sexy even with the hint of playfulness. "I want us in your bed the first time, not on a couch that you put together with an Allen wrench and picture instructions." She smiled a mischievous smile. "Not that I don't trust your prowess with tools."

He gently pulled the coat out of her grasp and threw it in the same direction he had tossed his own. He grasped the back of her neck and pulled her in for a brief, hard kiss. When he was done with that, he took her hand and turned toward the hall to his bedroom. She didn't want their first time to be on a couch and suddenly, neither did he.

Olivia

Kyle clicked on the lamp sitting on the bedside table

and bent, gently lifted the big gray cat out of the space between the pillows of his gigantic California king bed. He cradled the cat in his massive forearms, stroking its head. He didn't speak to the cat, but his hands on the pet told her everything she needed to know—this man was not just any man. He might be *her* man. The one she wanted, needed, had looked and waited for.

It had only been a few weeks and one exceptionally long date since they had connected. But Olivia Frances Hudson was going to be thirty-seven on her birthday in a few weeks. She wasn't seventeen anymore. She trusted herself enough to know what was starting to take root in her heart was not infatuation with a man who had tattoos and a Harley. She knew his people, she knew where he came from, and she knew his history. She had shared hers with him. They were not kids, and they had common roots that went deep into the Tennessee dirt.

She stood there, in the middle of his bedroom floor, while he took gentle care of his cat, and came to a life decision. She might be setting herself up for a catastrophe. Kyle made her feel safe and cared for, and those could be dangerous things to get used to.

"One is regret and self-pity and guilt and a bunch of other negative shit. The other one is serenity and grace and hope, and all the shit that makes us worthy of higher thinking. The wolf who will win the fight is the one you feed."

She was not feeding the bad one anymore.

The door clicked shut behind him when he returned to the room. He did not immediately come to her as she expected. Instead he leaned back against the doorjamb,

folded his arms on his chest, and surveyed her. Aware-
ness thrummed through the air between them.

"Second thoughts?" His words surprised her.

She didn't hesitate because there was nothing to
hesitate about. "Nope."

"You know this is not just gonna be fucking, right?"

Relief warred with something she couldn't exactly
name. "Yep."

He was silent for a minute. Just stood there, looking
at her. She held his gaze steadily. He continued after the
pause.

"Time to fish or cut bait, Olivia Mae. We both know
the road we're on. I'm good with the potholes we're
gonna hit. I just need to know you are gonna hold on
with me. Because I'm too old to go through getting my
heart broken again."

Tears sprang to her eyes at his words. They might
have sounded silly or melodramatic, especially coming
from this mountain of a man, this outwardly tough guy.
They didn't. They didn't because he meant them. They
were beautiful because they came from his heart and he
was letting her see it. He wasn't flowery. He was real.

This was a man who had sat in the freezing cold at
the side of his wife's fresh grave every night for nearly a
month.

A man who kept a kitchen table because it was a
good memory.

A man who lived with his heart and his soul right out
there for everyone to see.

She thought that her father would have liked him,
and the notion sent the tears rolling down her face.

"I can't promise I won't get scared. But I can promise I'll hold on, and I can promise I won't break your heart, honey." She brushed a hand over her cheek to get rid of the tears. "How is this happening so fast?"

He pushed from the door and came to stand in front of her, pulling her in for one his bear hugs. He smelled faintly of leather and the remnants of cold outdoor air.

"I don't know, baby. Probably happens a lot when people go on forty-eight-hour dates that include psychotic people and good barbecue."

She smiled against his shirt, and his voice lowered. She felt his chin come to rest on the top of her head. "I don't know how it's happening so fast, but I ain't questioning. For me, it just is. I think it is for you too. If you look at it from another way, it ain't so fast. It started in a parking lot twenty years ago."

She hugged him as tight as he held her, her arms wrapped around him. "You told me I had no, uh, tits."

"Well, that may have been true at the time. But I think things have changed since then."

He started to walk toward the bed, taking her with him as he went. Just before they got there, he twisted around and sat down on the edge of the mattress, holding her so she was standing in front of him. In this position, their faces were level. He drew her between his spread thighs with his hands on her hips.

"Let's get you naked, shall we? I need to do a comparison."

She shivered as his hands moved to slide up over her rib cage under her sweater, and before she could say a word, the sweater was over her head and somewhere on the floor of the room. Then she was in front of him in just a lacy blue bra. She expected more joking, but instead she watched his face, and his eyes didn't move from hers. His expression was serious.

"I'm sorry, Olivia. Sorry that I hurt you back then. I can't promise I won't ever do it again. But I can promise it won't be your heart that takes the hit."

Olivia held his eyes, reached to the front clip, and released her bra, swiftly peeling it down her arms. Without losing his eyes, she moved her hand and pulled one of his from her hip to mold it to one of her breasts. Immediately his hard, cool fingers tightened around the soft mound. She caught her breath and took a small step forward. She reached to put her hands on his shoulders.

"Time to fish or cut bait, big guy."

CHAPTER 13: ONE HELL OF A SIGHT

Kyle

She had too many fucking clothes on.

The sweater was gone. The bra was gone. He didn't have a memory of exactly what had been going on when she was a teenager, but what was in front of him now was magnificent. Soft, warm, substantial slopes dusted with freckles and crowned with nipples that made his mouth water. She stood proudly, letting him look at her body, and her confidence was enough to make his dick jerk. He bent to her, unable to resist, flicking his tongue out to taste.

She sucked in a breath and whispered, "Yes."

Her response was all the encouragement he needed to open his mouth and take one deep. She whimpered and he sucked hard, using one hand to lift her and hold her to his lips. He put his other hand to the zipper of her jeans, fumbling slightly because his mouth was on a trip to heaven. He felt her fingers at the fastening, helping him. He left her to deal with it and moved the hand to her other breast, palming it and rubbing his thumb across the bud. She gasped and he pulled hard, gently biting, and she rewarded him with a little cry. He released her flesh and trailed his tongue across her chest to the other breast. There he teased with his tongue tip, squeezing with his hand.

She grasped on to his biceps at either arm, moaning another, "Yes." Kyle reached to see what the status was of her zipper and was pleased to find the fly open. He closed his mouth over her second breast and moved to push down her jeans and panties to her thighs.

His lips were at her nipple and he whispered, "Open your legs for me." He pulled the tip of her breast into his mouth at the same time he slid his hand between her legs. She whimpered louder.

Jesus, she was hot. He stroked the top of her crease with a finger and she bucked slightly. He increased the suction at her breast and probed, increasing the pressure until he was sure he had found her clit. He circled his finger slightly and one of her hands grasped the back of his head, another of those little whimpers escaping from her mouth. He released her breast and looked up at her face. Her eyes were closed. He pushed with his finger, trying to get deeper.

"Wider, baby. Give me more." He felt her legs push against the inside of his thighs. There wasn't a lot of room, but she managed to give him more. He pulled her mouth down to him and pushed his tongue into the wet heat of it at the same time he slid his finger deep. Her legs buckled and he held her up with one arm, while he plundered her mouth and finger fucked her deep. She was amazingly tight, deliciously hot, and Kyle felt his head start to swim as his cock swelled painfully behind his own fly.

He wanted a taste of that deliciousness and he was not going to deprive himself any longer. He stroked deep then slid his hand out of her panties and released her mouth. He stood and held her steady for a moment before twisting and reversing their positions. Going to his knees in front of her and grabbing one of her legs, he found and pulled down the long zippers on her knee-length boots. Removing them, he tossed them aside, then reached for the waistband of her jeans, jerking them and her panties down her long legs.

Fucking hell, those legs.

While he was doing this, Olivia had reclined back on her elbows, watching him. Her eyes were heavy, sultry, hot. She was the sexiest thing he'd ever seen.

Ever.

In his life.

He didn't feel any guilt about thinking that because it was the honest to Christ truth. When he had her naked, he stood in front of her, taking it all in. Her breasts were full and still flushed from his mouth. Her stomach was mostly flat, but softly rounded. There was a smattering of freckles pretty much everywhere, and his fingers itched to map every single one.

Especially the ones that were scattered over and between her thighs. Her pussy had a cute little landing strip of coppery hair, and he grinned to himself. They were gonna discuss that in fine detail at some point. But right now, he wanted his face between those freckled thighs. Then he wanted those magnificent fucking legs wrapped around his back.

"You have too many clothes on."

Her voice brought his attention away from contemplating her pussy. He moved his eyes slowly back up her body, leisurely and with purpose, letting her see his admiration of it before he met her eyes again.

"I'm gonna need you to get all that off, big guy. Time's a wastin' and I need to see that leprechaun tattoo." She didn't move from her reclining position, except to push up farther on her elbows.

Kyle reached back with both hands, grasping the shirt between his shoulder blades and pulling it and the tee shirt under it over his head, chucking them both aside. He toed off his boots; at the same time he was unbuttoning and unzipping his fly. He nearly groaned in relief when his cock sprang free. He straightened, finally as naked as she was, and he saw that her eyes on him were round and her mouth had fallen open slightly.

Christ Almighty, a man could lose his shit over a woman looking at him like that. The look in her eyes briefly sidetracked him, and he wondered if she felt the same when had taken his visual trip up her body.

He hoped so.

Olivia

The sight of his body was her undoing.

First was the ink. She didn't know where the leprechaun was, but it wasn't on his chest or arms. Across one massively muscled shoulder, angling from his collarbone to his rib cage and covering the top of his pectoral and bicep, was a phoenix. The entirety of one wing was splayed across his pectoral, but the angle of it told her that the other wing continued onto his shoulder and back. The swirls of its wings and feathers were a burst of colors, and flames meshed and surrounded it. It was intricate and detailed and breathtaking. She couldn't imagine how long it must have taken to have it done.

From just below his elbow to just before his wrist on the same arm was the face of a clock, the numbers done in an intricate, old-fashioned script. There were vines and flowers twined around and through the hands of the clock. The hands were pointed at seven ten.

His other arm was a full sleeve from shoulder to wrist. From the top of his bicep to just past the bend of his elbow were drawings of trees, the branches gnarled and intertwined. There was no color. The artist had relied on shading and angles and curves to depict a forest that looked both beautiful and subtly chilling. Past his elbow the forest devolved into a pile of logs, against which a wooden mask, the detail exquisite, was nestled. From one eye ran a stream of blood red, from the other eye a stream of black twisted in rivulets down the face of the mask.

The art on his body was beautiful and they made his remarkable physique even more amazing. She kept drinking him in and he stood there, letting her. His chest and arms could crush her; his thighs were thick and heavily muscled. And his cock.

Dear Lord, his cock.

Thick and long and perfectly crowned, it stood proud as evidence of his desire for her. She swallowed and raised her eyes from his length to his face.

"You are beautiful."

She watched the fire flare in his eyes, and he moved to the bed, looming over her. "Baby, there is nothing more beautiful than you are, right here and right now."

Then she watched as he knelt on the floor. He put his hands to her knees and pushed them apart, and the pulse between her legs pounded hard and hot. She stayed up on her elbows and held his gaze, while he bent and put his tongue to the skin of her inner thigh. His eyes burned into hers as he moved his head, sucking and licking his way down toward his goal. When his mouth found the skin at the bend of her leg, he nipped and sucked harder, so close to where she wanted him to be.

"Honey, please..." She was going to reach down and drag his mouth to her if he didn't hit the goal soon. She felt him blow on the target and she whimpered, "Please, Kyle. God, please."

He was on her. Her head fell back to the bed, and she arched her hips up for him. He stroked the seam with the tip of his tongue; then he opened her with his fingers, unmasking the pulsing nub of muscle and nerves for his mouth. He flicked with his tongue, then he drew her clit in and sucked hard, and her back left the bed. A small part of her brain registered his big hand flattening on her lower belly to hold her in place, but she wasn't in control enough to care about it. She was unraveling and there was no stopping it.

"Kyle, baby, it's coming. I can't... Honey..." Her strangled, incoherent words were barely decipherable.

He bore down on her, his lips and teeth and tongue voracious, at the same time he slid two fingers deep.

There was no time to warn him further. Olivia felt her body erupt in pleasure, her back bowing, her lower body straining against his hand where it held her. Her orgasm was mighty, hard, and long, the muscles of her pussy clasping his fingers. She might have cried out, but she wasn't entirely sure. The waves of it kept rolling through her and he kept his fingers deep insider her, probing and thrusting smooth and strong. He laved the folds of her pussy with his tongue, staying with her as they both rode her orgasm to its end.

Finally, she felt herself settling, the ripples of heat and pleasure subsiding. She hadn't completely relaxed when he moved, and she let out a noise somewhere between a gasp and a small scream when he flexed the fingers inside her, pushed firmly and deeply then slid them out. He stood and bent to her, lapping at the indentation of her navel, dragging his mouth across her midriff and up between her breasts to the hollow at the center of her collarbones. He joined her in the bed and pulled her on top of him. His fingers finished pulling the twists of the long-forgotten braid out of her hair, and he tangled his fingers in the curls. Pulling her face down to him, he murmured against her lips.

"Now that was one hell of a sight."

His mouth was hot, his lips burning, his tongue thrusting and hard as he kissed her. She was the one to break it. Moving to reach down his body, she opened her mouth over the skin of his chest, flicked a flat nipple with her tongue, and told him, "Big guy, you ain't seen nothin' yet."

She wanted to take him in nearly every way a woman

could take a man. She stroked and licked and caressed. She whispered to him how much she liked his chest and his hands and his arms. Sliding her tongue up the side of his corded neck, she purred into his ear how hot she thought his tats were. Her mouth and hands were everywhere. Well, nearly everywhere. She waited to touch his cock until it was a fever in her to do so. But when she scooted farther down his body, her intention to take him in her mouth clear, he curled up and put his hands under her arms. He pulled her back up his body, then flipped her to her back and put his mouth to hers, growling low.

"Not this time, baby. If you put that mouth anywhere close to my dick, it will be all over but the crying. I want to come inside that hot little pussy tonight. Plenty of time for extracurriculars later."

She giggled into his mouth. "Isn't what you just did an, um, extracurricular?"

He nipped at her bottom lip and pulled her outside leg up to wrap it around his hip, pushing a big thigh between hers and up, until the wet heat between her legs was pressed into his skin. The roughness of the hair there felt delicious and she rubbed herself against it. God, she had just had the granddaddy of all orgasms. How could she want him again already?

His mouth was moving on the skin of her neck and throat, and he spoke through this activity. "That was just an appetizer, as it were. We're about to have the entrée, the side dishes, and dessert, baby."

He pushed his thigh higher and she ground down on to it. His growled, "Yeah, baby, that's it" shot through her, and she reached to clutch his ass, wanting him closer, wanting him inside. He brought his mouth back to hers, kissing her hot and wet and fierce. His hand slid between their bodies, and she gasped against his mouth when he slid a finger over the ultra-sensitized flesh there.

"You ready, sweetheart? Because damn, you feel wet and ready to me." He rose up and looked down at her, first her face, then down to where his hand cupped her. "I am so ready for this sweet little thing. You ready to do this?" His finger slid into her, taking some of the wetness that drenched her there, and moving it back to her clit. He pressed and circled, and she dug her head back into the mattress.

She panted out her answer. "God, Kyle, yes. I want you inside me now, honey."

He leaned over her and reached a long arm to the bedside table. Coming back with a packet, he moved to kneel between her now-splayed legs. His eyes holding hers again, he ripped the foil with his teeth, threw it away toward the table, and reached down to roll on the condom, his eyes never leaving hers.

Then, without speaking and without breaking their stare down, he bent, put his hands to her hips, and pulled her body to him. In one smooth move, using the muscles in his arms and chest and the sheer raw power of his upper body, he moved her entire frame—all five feet nine inches, one hundred and forty-three pounds of her—positioning her pelvis up until it rested on his thighs. She clutched the sheet with her hands.

Holy shit!

She kept her eyes glued to his, hoping he could read

in hers what she knew she could read in his. She was more turned on than she'd ever been in her life. She wanted him inside her so deep that it felt like he was a part of her body. She wanted to see and feel him come deep in her pussy. She wanted it more than she wanted her next breath.

"Here we go, Olivia Mae."

She felt him position the tip of his cock at her entrance, and she pushed her hips up. "Fish or cut bait, big guy." She barely recognized her own voice.

He flexed his hips and in one long, slow, excruciatingly sweet, breathtakingly powerful stroke, he was inside her to the hilt.

CHAPTER 14: ELEPHANTS AND POTHOLES

Kyle

For the first time since he was a teenaged punk, he had to force himself not to come.

Kyle had slept with more than his fair share of women before Aponi. When he was married, they had a frequent and adventurous sex life. He was no rookie between the sheets. But he hadn't been bullshitting when he told Olivia he would come if she put his dick in her mouth. He had to grit his teeth to keep from shooting when he hit bottom in her tight, soaked pussy. She was so wet, so scorching; it was so unbelievably good. Squeezing his eyes shut and holding himself still deep inside her, he didn't dare move for a minute.

She wrapped both her legs around his waist, and he buried his face in her neck, groaning as he slid in another impossible inch.

"Jesus fuck, Livie. So fucking good, baby. You feel so fucking good." He didn't recognize his own voice.

"Mmmmm..." The sound she made vibrated through her body and he relished the feeling against his skin.

They stayed still, locked together. Then he couldn't stay still any longer. Anchoring one hand in the bed, he cupped one of her breasts with the other and came down, opening his mouth over hers. He drew his hips back and thrust back in.

Christ. So good.

He did it again, faster this time. Then faster still, beginning to pump into her. She bent her knees and raised her thighs, gripping him along his waist and sides.

Fucking fantastic.

He undulated his hips and pushed in hard from a different angle. He was gratified when she cried out, "Honey..." dragging her mouth from his.

He had to go and he had to go harder, faster. "You with me, baby?" He moved his hand from rubbing her nipple to between her legs, finding her clit. She cried out again, her voice strangled and uneven.

"Baby, you with me?" He felt the clutching of her pussy walls and he pumped faster, slamming his pelvis into hers. Jesus, he felt like his balls were going to detonate.

"I'm with you. Harder, honey. More." He felt her nails dig into the skin of his shoulders.

More he gave her. He gave her everything, and when he felt the ripples deep inside her start, when she cried out his name, he slammed into her once, twice, three times. On the fourth stroke he exploded, molten heat crashing from the base of his spine, his balls, his entire body suffused with it. Her body milked his, clenching and squeezing as he shot deep, his hips jerking with his orgasm. He heard his own grunted groans, and God help him, but it was the most intense orgasm of his life. Nothing even came close. His hips kept thrusting involuntarily, the hot spurts of his release seeming never to end.

Finally, her legs slid down to rest on the bed and he slumped on top of her. Just for a few seconds, he needed to catch his breath, to reset the planet that had tipped off its axis. He forced himself to push his weight off her and he anchored his arm on the bed beside her. Her magnificent breasts where heaving slightly, the nipples flushed and hard, her eyes were closed, her lips were parted, ruby red and swollen from his kisses. Christ, she was beautiful.

His own breathing was still slightly labored, and he felt a trickle of sweat roll down his stomach. He took a deep breath to steady himself and the scent of the room hit him. It was sultry and sweet. It was sex and heat and this woman. If she hadn't just wrecked him, he would have gone at her again. Unable to resist, he bent his head and nuzzled one of her breasts with his nose, sliding just the tip of his tongue out to taste, tracing a path of those hot as fuck freckles to the summit.

He felt her move to clasp the back of his head and lightly hold him to her.

"Big guy, I'm gonna need a minute. My body won't survive another orgasm right now."

He chuckled against her skin. "Are you doubting my powers, Frances?"

"I would never. But since one of us is human—and

I'm pretty sure it's me—I would really like it if I didn't need to go to the hospital tonight."

He rolled to his side next to her, pulling her into his arms and reaching for the blanket that was folded at the end of the bed. Pulling it over her, tucking it around her sides. Then he reached to the pillows and pulled two over to where they lay mostly crossways in the big bed.

"Up," he instructed.

She complied and he shoved a pillow under her head, being careful not to pull her hair.

"Be back. Gotta deal with the condom."

He did so, washed his hands, and returned to the bed. She pushed up on an elbow and hauled back the blanket, making a place for him beside her. That felt good, her making a place for him. He put a knee to the mattress and moved back to her side.

Reaching for another pillow, he shoved it under his own head, then repositioned her down the length of his side and rested a hand on her naked ass under the cover. He bent his other arm and folded it behind his head. He liked that she moved right into him, laying her head on his chest, just under his chin, and placing her hand flat-palmed on his stomach. This was good. Outside of the unprecedented way he had just come, this was the best part of the last two days. Holding Olivia against him, the feeling she belonged there, seeping into his bones.

"You okay, big guy?" She sounded just a trace nervous. He knew why. It was a pothole, and it was a significant one. He knew this because he knew what he would be thinking if the roles were reversed.

But he was not bringing Aponi into their bed. She had no place there, and if she were alive, she would have agreed. They would deal with it, because he was not going to allow the elephants to take over the room.

But not here and not now.

Here and now was theirs. So he unfolded his arm from under his head, reached across his chest and put his fingers under her chin. He tipped her face up to his and kissed her softly. Then he held her eyes as he told an absolute truth.

"I have never been better, Olivia. Never."

Olivia

She came awake slowly, confused at first about where she was. The pillow under her head was softer than she was used to, and she was naked. She moved her legs and turned to her back. The area between her legs protested slightly. Remembering last night and why she had a slight soreness there, she smiled and looked across the bed. There was a gaggle of pillows, a quilt in addition to the blanket she was currently under, but she was alone.

Well, not really. Sitting regally amongst the pillows, leisurely grooming a leg, was Beast. At her movement he looked up from his chore, regarded her like the commoner she was, and went back to his task.

Well, then.

Cats.

They classified all other living beings as enemies, peasants, or staff. Even the ones who were friendly had agendas. She had become familiar with probably hundreds of them over the years, and nothing had changed her opinion of the feline life-form. They attacked you if you gave them the wrong kind of shit, sucked up to you if they wanted something they couldn't get on their own, or ignored you.

Olivia liked cats because they had attitude and they were beautiful. But she was not a cat person, per se. She preferred blind adoration and a little bit of a mess to her pets, which was why she had a dog. Snape was loyal, loving, hopelessly devoted to her, and needed nothing more in life than to serve and get bacon occasionally.

But Beast was a gorgeous animal, and his sumptuous gray fur begged to be stroked. Therefore, she put a hand out toward him, tutting in a soft voice as she did so.

"Hey there, gorgeous. Are going to rip me to shreds if I touch you?"

The big cat looked at her, put down his leg, stood, turned, walked to the edge of the bed, and jumped with soft plop to the floor. He leisurely walked to the open door and exited the room, his tail held up and waving in disdain. He didn't acknowledge the presence of the man standing in the open doorway.

"Told you he was an asshole."

She watched him come fully into the room. He was wearing a pair of gray sweatpants and a long-sleeved white tee shirt. He carried a steaming mug in each hand. The curls at the top of his head were messy and his cheeks were dark with stubble. He looked good enough to eat.

"If that is coffee, you might be the greatest man to ever exist."

She sat up, holding the blanket to her chest. It was chilly in the room, and she could see frost on the edges of the window in the wall across from the bed. When the air hit her back, goosebumps shivered across her skin. Kyle wordlessly handed her a mug, set the other down on the table by the bed, and moved to open a drawer in the enormous wooden chest that rested against the wall beside the window. He pulled out the twin to the shirt he had on and moved to the bed. Sitting down next to her, he took the cup from her hands, handed her the shirt, and gestured with his hand.

"Put this on. It's cold in here."

She frowned slightly at his tone but did as he instructed. She didn't mind the alpha male attitude that had been taking care of her for the last two days. It had been nice to simply let Kyle take charge and take care of things. But Olivia was not a person who liked to be bossed around, and the timbre of his voice didn't sit well. Uncomfortably, she also noticed that he wasn't teasing her, he didn't kiss her, and it was the first time he didn't meet her eyes when she looked at him.

"Is everything all right?" She would give him a chance. But dread and a dark feeling she didn't want to identify, crept into her chest.

He got up from the bed and reached for his mug. "Yeah. I just have some shit to take care of."

Then he turned away from the bed and walked out of the room. He still didn't meet her eyes, and the dread deepened. Ignoring the mug on the table, she yanked the shirt over her head, climbed out of his bed, and headed across the hall to the guest room. Once there, she grabbed clothes and her toiletry bag. She took a shower, braided her hair, dressed, and walked out to the living area.

Snape and Kyle were gone.

CHAPTER 15: CRATERS

Kyle

Kyle stood at the entrance to the large breed enclosure at the dog park that was a quarter of a mile from his rental. Snape was lumbering after a golden retriever and Kyle was on his cell. The text he had received at six thirty that morning still made his blood boil.

"Call me, motherfucker."

He had gotten out of the house and done just that. He had known exactly who it was, even if the number hadn't identified the asshole. There was only one person with the reservation area code who fit the bill.

"Now you show up out of the blue, three years later, and word is you're screwing some fancy white bitch vet."

The venom in the man's voice coming out of the cell was familiar, even if Kyle hadn't heard it in a while. It wasn't a pleasant familiarity. Ray Blankenship had hated Kyle for as long as Kyle had hated him. Their relationship had started out bad, on the day Kyle had to bodily take his future mother-in-law out of her house because she couldn't walk on her own well enough to leave. It had deteriorated from there.

Ray Blankenship.

Aponi's father.

Kyle turned and walked to the far side of the enclosure. There were only a couple of people at the park this early on a decidedly nippy Sunday morning, but he didn't want anyone to hear what was sure to be a nasty conversation. He didn't wonder how Ray had heard about Olivia. The man might live on the reservation, but news and gossip had a way of circulating fast in Faithful's neck of the country.

"What do you want, Ray?"

Kyle wasn't going to waste time listening to the litany of shit and excuses Raymond Blankenship always listed about why his life was fucked. He didn't even need to ask what he wanted. Aponi's old man wanted what he always wanted—money. Specifically, he wanted what he considered to be his cut of the insurance money Kyle had gotten when Aponi was killed. Kyle had left Faithful and moved to Florida because he had needed to get away from the place where everywhere he looked reminded him of what he had lost.

He also left because Ray Blankenship had decided to make Kyle's life a living hell. The man had hired a hack lawyer and tried to use tribal law to get the money. It hadn't worked. He hired the same hack lawyer to try to sue Jake Beckett for wrongful death, since Aponi was killed in his clinic. That hadn't worked either. Finally, he had tried to intimidate members of Kyle's family, specifically his aunt, Rhonda, into persuading Kyle to give him a cut of the money.

Big mistake that had been.

Aunt Rhonda had taken her Glock 22, pulled Ray's ass off the lunch counter stool at Casey's Diner, and made her case for him to cut the shit. She had done this after she frog-marched him into the kitchen of the diner and shoved the man face first into the tile wall beside Casey's wife's pie case. Ray had seen the error of his ways, slunk back to the reservation with a broken nose, and Kyle had gotten on his bike and escaped to the Gulf of Mexico.

The man's voice was as nasty as Kyle's memory recalled, and it had him considering the merits of dunking his relatively new iPhone in a vat of disinfectant when the call was over.

"I want what's mine, motherfucker. What you stole, and what is rightfully mine, you son of a whore. I'm in this stinking rathole while you're living it up on the back of my daughter? I don't fucking think so. Did you really think I was just gonna let it go, motherfucker?"

Now, it seemed, he had refortified his dedication to the cause. Unfortunately for him, Kyle had less sympathy for the man now than he ever had. Fuck. He should be piled up in bed with Olivia, with his hands on her ass, and his tongue in her mouth.

Fuck. Kyle took a slow deep breath. Now he was gonna have to call his lawyer in Knoxville and give Rhonda a heads-up. At this exact moment, he was going to be required to deal with shit that was going to put a damper on what had been shaping up to be one fantastic fucking Sunday.

Fuck.

He took another deep breath and dealt with the immediate shit.

"Listen to me, Ray, because I'm only gonna say this once. You gave up any claim to anything of Aponi's the first time you took a hand to her. I don't give a planetary fuck if you are sleeping in a ditch on the side of 321 and eating dog turds for breakfast. Lose this number. Lose any number of anybody I might possibly know. If you call this number again for any goddamn reason, I'm gonna make it my business to see that your sorry ass is living in a fucking cardboard condo under a bridge some-where, you hear me? And if you bother Rhonda again, I'm gonna let her give you an enema with that Glock she loves so much."

The man sputtered in Kyle's ear, "You son of a bitch, I'll..."

Kyle interrupted him. "You'll do fuck. You'll do fuck because you're a coward. It's over. It's been over. I've dealt with your shit for the last time. You're an old man who beat his kids and his wife, who can't hold down a job, and who squandered away whatever life he could have had. You want money? Get a tin cup."

Kyle hit the disconnect button the screen of his phone. Sometimes it just felt good to tell an asshole to go fuck himself. He stood in the park for a while, letting his temper cool to a slow simmer.

Then he whistled for Snape.

Olivia

She wasn't going to lose her temper and she wasn't going to cry.

Olivia had spent the last half hour repacking her overnight bag and making the bed in the guest room. These things she did after she called Laura Beckett and asked if she could spend a few days with her. She explained about what had happened, matter-of-factly, keeping her voice neutral. She didn't say where she was or who she was with. She probably would talk to Laura about Kyle, but not until she figured out how she was going to deal with the fact she had made one monumental mistake in sleeping with him.

In the last forty-five minutes, which was how much time had lapsed since Kyle walked out of the bedroom, the pothole had become a crater. Unable to recognize her insecurities for what they were, Olivia had convinced herself Kyle had behaved the way he had this morning because he regretted what had happened. Or maybe he just felt guilty because of what they had shared. Either way, it didn't matter. Thinking she could have all of him was a mistake.

She failed to stop and examine the validity of what she was feeling. She didn't check the freight train of unreasoned fear that barreled into her gut. She missed the warning signs that a year of counseling had taught her so well to see. She ignored the spiral of self-doubt and anxiety. Three days of emotional calisthenics laid waste to her coping skills, and the fear slammed into her psyche with such force it nearly took her to her knees.

Entangled with this emotional shitstorm was the aftermath of the break-in at her house. All of it together was just too much, too close together. She reached out unsteadily for one of the green chairs at the table and sat down before she fell down. Her legs were suddenly shaking so hard, her entire body shaking so violently, her teeth were chattering. A panic attack the likes of which she hadn't had since college gripped her. She put her head down nearly to her knees and struggled to keep her breathing shallow and even. She wasn't successful. She heaved in great mouthfuls of air and her fingers started to tingle.

Oh God, oh God.

She couldn't breathe, couldn't think. The room seemed to tilt, and her heart felt like it was going to explode.

She didn't hear him come in the door, and she didn't feel Snape nudge her leg with his cold, wet nose. The first thing she became aware of, other than the waves of dread and physical horror that washed through her, was Kyle's voice and his hands on her upper arms.

"Olivia, what's wrong?" He had squatted down in front of her and he shook her gently when she didn't answer but kept gulping in oxygen. "Baby, what the fuck?"

"I can't...panic attack..." The four words were all she could manage. Every coping mechanism she had ever learned flew from her memory. There were only the waves of unreasoning terror roiling through her.

She didn't protest when Kyle stood, bent, and picked her up in his arms. He walked with her to the couch and sat down, cradling her in his arms. She heard his deep voice, elevated to make himself heard over her loud pants as she struggled to bring more air into lungs that were already saturated to bursting with oxygen.

"Slow down, Olivia. Focus on my voice and slow down, baby." In a detached way, she felt a hand on the back of her head gently push her face toward her lap.

"Focus, baby, and slow it down. Count, Livie. Count with me. One, inhale." He paused for a few seconds. "Two, exhale."

"I can't, Kyle. I can't breathe. I..."

His hand moved to hold her at the back of her neck, his fingers firm but gentle. "Come on, Olivia. Slow. Focus. One and in." She latched on to the arm that held her around her waist with both hands, her knuckles white. "Two and out. Come on, baby. You can do this."

His voice became a mantra and she focused on just his words, doing what he told her to do. It felt like hours, but the tingling in her fingertips finally lessened then stopped altogether. Gradually, but steadily, she became aware that the shaking had ebbed. She stopped feeling as though she was suffocating, or she might fly into a million pieces. The reality that she was not going to faint, die, or lose control took root.

"That's it, baby. That's it. Relax. It's almost over." His palm felt warm through the fabric of her shirt, as it began a slow and steady massage of her lower back.

Finally, she took in a shuddering breath and blew it out, then slumped into Kyle's arms. Her rational brain started to reassert itself. Automatically, even after years, her affirmative self-talk kicked in, just like she had practiced for so long so many years ago.

It had been a big one. It had been ugly and awful. It had been insidious, triggered when she hadn't been prepared. For a moment, it had controlled her, but she had survived and taken it down. It was over, and she was fine. Nothing extreme had happened. She had once again conquered an everyday monster that millions of people battled daily. She flexed her fingers and looked down to see that they looked normal. It was over and she had won.

Except Kyle had witnessed it, and knowing he had took a giant edge off her victory.

She felt the strength of him surrounding her, and it felt wonderful, but it also made her squirm inside with humiliation. She did not want him to see her like that, not ever, but most especially not today.

"How long have you had the attacks, Livie?" His voice was calm, but it held a wealth of warmth and concern. She turned her face into his chest. She didn't want to answer, didn't want to share the weakness she was trying to fight and hide.

His arms tightened their hold around her. "Baby, I'm a nurse. I know what an anxiety attack is, and I know how real they are."

He moved an arm, and the rough pads of his fingers smoothed her hair back from her cheekbone and the side of her face. She settled her body against his chest. The sense of relief she felt at his words of validation couldn't be minimized. She felt a physical weight lift. Maybe he wouldn't take this as a sign she was a woman he might not want to take on. But the thought, the doubt, was unworthy of him.

And of her.

"How long, sweetheart?"

She swallowed hard and answered. "Years. I was diagnosed in vet school, but the attacks have been happening since I was twelve." She swallowed hard again and continued, "They started a few months after my mother died."

"Do you take anything for them?" His hand on the small of her back moved up to circle the area between her shoulders.

"Not now. I always hated taking medication. I know it makes no sense, given what I do, but I wanted to be strong enough not to have to depend on a pill. I spent a little over a year in therapy, learning how to manage the anxiety."

She paused briefly in the narrative. The flaw in her reasoning was obvious. Not for the first time, she chastised herself for allowing such self-indulgent ignorance. Hell, it wasn't ignorance. It was purposeful avoidance of an approved treatment for a valid condition.

He was silent for a moment and she knew what he was thinking. "Olivia, you know..."

She stopped him. "I know. I should take the meds. Today is plenty of evidence that I am still weak."

In one swift and smooth move she was on her back on the couch, and Kyle was looming over her. For the first time she saw anger in his eyes that was directed at her. She had only had a few brief glimpses of his temper so far, but this was not a glimpse. He was pissed at her.

His hand gripped her jaw, and it was tight. His eyes were blazing into hers, and his voice was tense with his effort to control the volume and intensity of what he said next.

"Fucking hell, Olivia. You are not weak. You have a goddamned condition that requires treatment. Period. Is that what you would tell a client? That they were weak because their fucking dog had seizures? Seriously? Goddamn it!"

He squeezed his eyes tightly shut; then dropped his head until his forehead was leaning against the side of her face at her temple. She listened to his increased breathing and sensed he was working to calm down. She lay quietly and let him, bringing her hands up to stroke the short hair at the nape of his neck. God, this man was something else. He lifted his head after a few moments, and she was relieved to see the anger was gone.

"I'm sorry, Frances. I'm sorry." He blew through teeth in frustration.

"I had a call this morning that lit my fuse and listening to you spout stuff you know is bullshit set it off again. It's no excuse, though." He bent to her and placed a brief kiss on her cheek. "I'm sorry, baby."

He settled his forehead back to rest on hers, and they lay together in silence for a long time. She wanted to ask about his phone call but decided against it. She would, but not then.

"Do you want to talk about this anymore?"

Olivia knew they needed to, but the attack had exhausted her. "Not especially, no. You want to talk about that phone call?"

"Fuck, no."

He moved his head and brushed his lips across her mouth. "You hungry?" His breath was warm and smelled faintly of mint and coffee.

She considered his question. "Starving."

"Then let's go eat."

Kyle

He didn't want to talk about the call later, either.

He didn't want to talk about anything but how fucking good it felt to have her riding his dick while he leaned back against his headboard.

They had eaten lunch at Casey's, bought some groceries to take back to his house, watched a movie, and walked Snape back to the dog park. Olivia had spent about forty-five minutes trying to get Beast to stop being an asshole and let her hold him. She failed, but Kyle admired the effort she expended.

Sam had checked in via text, but there was really nothing pertinent to share. Then he and Olivia had talked about the logistics of everything that was happening the next day. She told him she had to go into the clinic, and he listened as she called her vet tech and arranged the time for them to meet at her office. She was not going to be alone. In addition to her vet tech, the cleaning company people were arriving two hours before she was going to be there and would be there all day long. Satisfied with those arrangements, he left Olivia to go back to wooing Beast while he sent a text to the answering service of the lawyer he used. He left a message, arranging for a meeting the next day. He needed to give the woman a heads-up about Ray Blankenship, and instructions on what to do if he decided to cause trouble.

Then he moved into the kitchen, stepping over Snape, who didn't move or wake up. Kyle turned his back to the living room where Olivia and Beast were having a come-to-Jesus meeting, and called Rhonda. In low tones he filled her in on his call from Ray Blankenship. Her reaction was what he expected.

"Are shitting with me? The fucker better get right with Jesus because next time it'll be something more consequential than his nose that gets busted. I'll hang his sorry ass wrinkled dick off a light pole."

That was Aunt Rhonda: delicate and refined in any given situation.

He snorted a laugh into the phone. "Now don't get the vapers, darlin'. Ray Blankenship is a gnat, and I'll let Janet Carlton swat him and he'll crawl back under his rock. No worries."

Rhonda Valentine's snort was not one of humor. "I got a machete in lockup that I've been dyin' to neuter a choice asshole with, but I didn't have a worthy candidate. Ray Blankenship would fit the bill simply fuckin' perfect." She paused, and Kyle sensed she had more to say. He was not wrong.

"Heard you're seein' Doc Hudson's girl."

"Yeah."

"You good?" The two words held a lot more that she wouldn't say out loud.

Kyle smiled. "Yeah."

She was silent again. He waited. "She's good people."

"Yeah, she is."

"Bring her over next Sunday. I'm making a ham. Bring some potatoes and some beer." There it was, the approval.

He smiled broader. "All right."

"And don't kill Charlie Barksdale. She's crazier than a shithouse rat, but she spent her life holed up with Abby Barksdale in that glorified pigsty, so it was inevitable."

"I'll try not. You done giving out motherly advice and counsel?"

"Kiss my country ass, boy. Don't forget the potatoes, and if you bring that cheap-ass beer you drink, I'll send your ass back to the liquor store before I feed you."

His phone signaled that the call disconnected.

After the call, he threw his cell on the counter, fired up the small grill he had bought that sat on the side porch of the house, and made steaks. Olivia made the salad from the supplies she chose at the Food Lion. They ate, cleaned up, and dealt with animals. Kyle decided it was turning out to be a decent day, all things considered.

It got a whole fuck of a ton better when a kiss in the kitchen turned into her hands around his dick and hearing her whisper that she wanted him to fuck her.

And here they were—Olivia on her knees, full of his cock, sliding slowly up and down. The sight of her was so goddamn hot he could have come just watching. The sweet clench of her pussy was tight enough to make his eyes roll back in his head, and when she undulated her hips, her hands in her hair and her eyes closed, he had to clamp his hands to her ass to maintain control.

He bent in to take a nipple, scoring with his teeth before pulling hard at the stiff peak. Her pace quickened and he groaned around the delicious mouthful. The inner walls of her tightness constricted hard on his cock and he was forced to release her tit.

"Jesus, baby, that's it. Fuck me hard."

She moved her hands to clutch at his shoulders, the tempo of her hips becoming harder and faster still, and she put her open lips on his. "So good." Her voice was thick with her arousal, the words hot in his mouth. "Your cock feels so good."

He needed her to come.

His balls were drawn up and his cock throbbed hard enough to be almost painful. He was close, and he knew she was too. Her movements were becoming uncoordinated, so he clamped a hand to her hip to help her take him. Leaning away from her slightly and holding her sultry gaze, he slid his long middle finger into his mouth. He moved the hand to her pussy and found her clit, massaging it with the same finger, and she whimpered and gasped.

"Kyle, oh God, Kyle..."

He thrust his tongue between her teeth, kissing her

deep, and felt the tiny ripples in her pussy become pulsating waves.

Olivia

When he slid the finger that had been in his mouth over her clit, she was gone.

She cried out his name and slammed her pelvis down on his, the staccato sounds of her orgasm escaped her lips, even as her hips jerked and thrust unevenly against him. She was coming hard, her entire body trembling in the wake, and she never wanted it to stop. The crushing tide of it went on and on, pounding waves of pleasure smashing through her body.

The intensity of it had just begun to recede when she heard him give a loud, long groan, and she barely had the presence of mind to watch the storm hit him. She was glad she did because the show was superb. The thick muscles of his neck arched his head back, and his teeth sank into his bottom lip. She felt the powerful muscles of his hips and thighs pump his cock up into her, his movements now uncoordinated and out of his control.

Clamping the walls of her sex onto him, she rode with him, and felt a second orgasm, less forceful but no less sweet, rise to surprise her. Gasping as the pulses of his orgasm intensified hers, by the time they both were coming down Olivia was convinced she was having an out-of-body experience.

He relaxed his grip on her hips and moved his hands and arms to pull her torso down on top of his. After-shocks flowed through her sex, and she heard his breath hiss between his teeth as he felt them, too.

"Holy shit, sweetheart."

Her breathing was still labored, and her body felt like jelly. "You're not kidding, big guy." She collapsed into his body and his "humpf" when she did so gave her not a nanosecond of concern. She had just fucked his, and her, brains out and had two orgasms. He would have to deal.

Besides, she didn't want to lose him just yet. She wanted to keep him there, deep inside, for as long as was humanly possible. Given the choice, she wanted him there forever. The thought sobered her. Notwithstanding her mental meltdown earlier, she considered herself to usually maintain a decent level of practicality. How practical, how wise, was it to be thinking these things? The answer was it wasn't practical. The wisdom of it might be up for debate, depending on which side of romance your bread was buttered on. The reality was, practical or not, she and Kyle Valentine were here, in this bed. For once in her life she was not going to overthink things.

But she had questions. Actually, she had one question. There might be potential follow-ups, but just one for the moment.

"Can I ask you something?" The words were out before her brain had given clearance.

"Am I gonna like the question?" There was a smile in his voice.

Fish or cut bait.

"I don't know. It's not what is your middle name."

"Thank Christ for that. Shoot."

"Do you think it's possible for us to just stay on this date and never really stop?"

He was quiet so long she thought he might not have heard. "Kyle?"

"You thought I had regrets this morning, didn't you?" She froze at his question.

"Kyle, I…" He didn't let her prevaricate.

"You did." It was a statement and no longer a question.

She sighed deeply. "Yes. How did you know?"

He tightened his arms around her. "Pothole, Olivia. I told you we were going to hit them, and what a more opportune moment than the morning after we first slept together."

"I'm sorry." She curved her arms around his neck and laid her head on his shoulder. "If you doubted me like that, it would gut me."

"If I thought you were comparing me to another man, it would gut me." He kissed the top of her head. "Potholes, baby."

They lay silently for a long while. She was getting drowsy when he spoke.

"You are not something I could ever regret, Olivia. I've been living with a knot in my gut for a long time, taking up so much room that I can hardly breathe. I loved before you. I can't, and do not want change that. But that knot, that load of love, that's now yours, sweetheart. Only yours. It's not secondhand, and it's not a leftover. It's brand spanking new, right off the showroom floor. Don't ever forget that."

He flexed his hips. "My cock is in you, baby, and I do not believe that it's just by chance. So whatever we gotta do to have this, we're gonna do it."

He pulled her head away from his shoulder and saw the tears sliding, dripping off her cheeks. He moved a massive, strong, gentle hand and wiped them away.

"So the answer is yes, as far as I am concerned, we can stay on our fucking first date until the end of time."

CHAPTER 17: AMBROSE

Olivia

He told her about Ray Blankenship over breakfast. She told him she already knew most of the bones of the story.

"How in the hell do you know all that shit?" His voice was ominous.

She had picked up a slice of toast and taken a bite before answering. "You do remember where we live, right? There isn't a soul in Faithful who doesn't consider Ray Blankenship a bastard for what he tried to do to you and Jake Beckett. Besides, Laura is my closest friend. Believe me, she has a truly clear opinion of Mr. Blankenship."

She fancied Kyle looked relieved when he realized he didn't have to narrate a history of Aponi's father. Pothole avoided, as it were. She was also happy to see that he didn't seem overly worried or show signs of being hassled. He had ushered Snape into his pickup, made sure she had everything she needed for the day, and taken her home.

Driving up the private road, she considered that she loved this pile of bricks and memories. She wondered idly how long she should wait before asking Kyle to live there with her.

At their present rate, Thursday would work.

She was relieved to see two box trucks and another truck with a trailer pulling what was most likely a vacuum device, with two huge gray tanks, parked in the side parking area by the clinic. Several men with green jumpsuits to match the color of the vehicles were moving with a purpose in and out of her house and around the trucks.

They parked and went into the clinic. Bryan was already there, computers humming and a sense of purpose about him, as well. Then Kyle had taken her into her office, pushed her up against the wall, and thoroughly kissed her.

"I'll be back and take you to lunch. Since it would not be fitting for me to fuck you up against this wall at the present time, and I gotta go see a lawyer." Then he slapped her rather rudely on her left butt cheek and left.

At eleven o'clock, Sam Beckett and Rhonda Valentine, of all people, had knocked on the clinic door. They had stayed just long enough for Rhonda to scare the hell out of Bryan, scratch Snape behind his ears, and ascertain that Olivia knew how to make potato salad.

"And don't put any goddamned pickles in it, for fuck's sake." Rhonda might have scared Olivia just a tad, as well.

Sam had grimaced, asked if she was okay and was anything amiss. She assured him all was as well as could be expected. They exited when Rhonda had walked to the door, looked at Olivia and said, "See you Sunday." Then she turned to Sam and ordered, "Let's go, boss. I ain't got all damn day." Olivia thought it was telling about who the boss actually was when Sam had followed her without another word.

At eleven fifteen Bryan said he was going to hit the fast food place down the road for a burger, and he would be back in an hour. He had been gone about five minutes when Olivia walked up the hall from her office, entered the large clinic area, and stopped dead in her tracks.

Charlie Barksdale was standing in the far corner of the room, one hand wrapped around Snape's leather collar and the other holding a butcher knife—with an eight-inch blade—poised at the side of the dog's furry neck.

"I need to see your father."

The words were as nonsensical as the woman's appearance. Iron gray hair stood out in matted clumps from her scalp. She wore loose-fitting overalls that might have once been white but were now streaked with all manner of stains. A long-sleeved dark blue sweatshirt showed under the straps of the overalls. Heavy black boots covered her feet and stopped at about mid-calf; the pant legs of the overalls stuffed into their tops. They were covered with what Olivia optimistically hoped was mud.

Olivia didn't remember her well enough to have a clear recollection of the woman's size. Charlotte Barksdale had her family's bulk and height. She was at least four or five inches taller than Olivia and outweighed her by at least twenty pounds. That explained how she had heaved the coyote up the back steps.

"I need to see your father now, or I'm sorry, but I'm gonna have to kill your dog," she wheedled, and she rocked slightly back and forth slightly.

Olivia's mind raced and the first grip of panic hit her stomach. She could not look at Snape. If she did, she might lose it.

"Ms. Barksdale, don't you remember? My father died four years ago." She watched as the woman's head tilted like a German shepherd hearing a police siren. "Why don't you give me that knife and we can sit down and talk?"

She had no idea what she would have done in the unlikely scenario of the woman just laying down the weapon. But it was a try.

Charlie twisted her hand and pulled Snape's head closer to her thigh. Olivia watched as his tongue lolled out of his mouth and he started to pant at the tightness around his neck.

"Get your father, bitch, or I am going to ram this knife straight through this mutt's gullet."

Olivia took a step forward, her hand out. "Charlie, I told you. My father died. It's not possible for me to get him for you. Please don't hurt my dog." She forced her voice to stay calm, even while her heart raced. "Snape is a good dog, Charlie. You like dogs. You don't want to hurt a dog. Please, just let him go and we can talk about whatever you need."

"You made them take my babies away." Her voice

raised in timbre, sounding almost like a child's. "My babies...babies...sweet little things..." The words were half-whispered in a singsong cadence as the woman tilted her head again. "Poor, sweet little things." Abruptly her voice was rough, and she jerked her head up, her eyes crazed and shooting malevolence at Olivia. "I had to put those two poor little things to sleep. Had to. Had to. You ignored the first one. You made me put them to sleep, yes you did, yes you did." She twisted Snape's collar harder and the dog coughed and began to wheeze. "Then I left you my gift. Happy birthday to you..." The singsong cadence was back.

Olivia watched as the woman began to sing under her breath, rocking from side to side and taking the choking, wheezing dog with her. She stopped singing abruptly and trained her malicious, insane gaze across the room. Olivia was frantically trying to inventory what was in the room she could use as a weapon, at the same time she weighed the risks of barreling across the room to save her dog. The woman might have twenty pounds on her but Olivia had sanity on her side, and she was at least fifteen years younger.

"Charlie, don't..."

"Frances, whose car..."

"Hey, Olivia, the cleaners want..."

In slow motion, it seemed, and nearly simultaneously, Bryan burst through the one set of swinging doors to the large exam/hospital room that came from the back of the clinic, and Kyle pushed through the others that led to the front hallway. Then, for the next two minutes, chaos reigned.

There were strangled shrieks from Charlie as she launched herself at Bryan, knife held high over her head.

Snape barked loudly and launched his big, furry body at Olivia, intent on getting to her to ask what the hell was going on.

Olivia screamed, "Kyle, look out!" as she watched, paralyzed, as he charged toward the screeching woman with the knife.

Kyle, for his part, was silent.

In two long strides, he was across the room. He pushed Bryan with one big arm and the gangly man went sprawling into a group of stainless-steel trays and stools. Pivoting on the balls of his feet, he deftly caught Charlie's arm as she brought down the butcher knife. She screamed, the sound shrill and inhuman, and bones cracking were audible as he twisted the arm holding the knife. The knife clattered to the floor amongst Bryan and all the stainless-steel instrument trays. Olivia watched in stupefied fascination, unable to take a breath, as Kyle took Charlie Barksdale to the floor, put a knee in her back, and pulled a set of handcuffs out of somewhere under the back of his jacket.

Handcuffs?

Kyle

"Do I want to know why you have handcuffs just sitting around in your pants?"

Sam and the uniforms had come and gone. They took Charlotte Winston Barksdale with them. Kyle had told them the woman might have a broken wrist, but further than that he did not give an eternal fuck.

Sam had slapped him on the back, shook his head,

told Olivia he would be in touch, and laughed all the way out to his county-issued SUV.

Bryan had declined an exam, stating he was fine, but he was going to hit the liquor store on his way home. He also told Olivia he would come in Wednesday to clean things up in the clinic. She started to protest. Kyle had interrupted and told Bryan he should do just that. She was no doubt going to give Kyle shit about being over-bearing, but he did not give a fuck about that, either.

He took her back to his rental, refused to answer about the handcuffs, and took her to bed. He made her come three times before midnight, fed her again, then tucked her under his arm, and they went to sleep for ten solid hours.

He stood at the railing on top of the observatory at Clingman's Dome, Olivia in front of him, staring out at the vista of the Smoky Mountains covered in a thin layer of snow. Directly in front of them but down several hundred feet, were two deer, noses to the ground as they foraged. He had her wrapped in her coat and pulled close to his body, so he could wrap her in his arms and pull the sides of his coat around her, too.

It was February. The observatory was closed, but Kyle knew a guy. The roads hadn't been bad, not with his chains, his four-wheel drive, and the fact he had been driving these highways in winter since he was fourteen.

They had now been on their first date for three months. Tomorrow he was moving his big screen and his cat into Olivia's kick-ass house, with the new kitchen island. But first he had to say something to her, and he wanted to say it here.

His favorite place in the world.

He wrapped her tighter in his arms and widened his stance to hold her as close as her could and protect her from the wind. He moved his head down until his lips were brushing the shell of her ear.

"Ambrose."

He felt her body still, and her breath suspend.

"It's Ambrose. And I love you, Frances."

Neither of them saw the two stars glow brighter for several seconds in the northeastern sky.

The man and the girl stood next to the headstone.

She was ten years old and her name was Gracie. Well, in totality, it was Grace Marlene Valentine. She was tall for her age, and she had freckles that she hated but her father loved. She played the violin and volleyball.

Her mother had taught her how to give her dog medicine and how to swim. Her father had taught her how to make Great Aunt Rhonda's potato salad. He had also taught her how to break someone's arm if she ever needed to, and that somebody named Eddie Van Halen was the greatest rock guitarist of all time.

Two days ago, her mother and father had both told her that her father had once been married before. They were telling her this now, they said, because she was no longer a little girl and they knew she would be able to understand. It had been hard, thinking about her tall, loud, handsome father—the man who danced in their kitchen and kissed her mother in front of her friends just to freak her out—being with someone else.

It had made her uncomfortable, and she told her dad so that morning on the way home from volleyball practice.

So he brought her here.

He had her sit criss-cross applesauce in front of him on the grass. He told her about being young, about how the woman had made him happy when he was young. He told her about the baby and how the woman had died.

She watched his face carefully. She couldn't stand having her father sad. But he didn't look sad. His eyes were soft, like when he had talked to her after she didn't make the competition team.

She had to ask him, though.

"Did you love her more than Mama?"

She watched him smile at her. She loved that feeling she got in her stomach when he smiled at her.

"No, baby. I did not love her more than Mama. It was different. Not more, not less. Just different. You see, we all have a never-ending supply of love. I gave her the love that was hers, and I give Mama the love that belongs to her." He had reached to push the hair out of her eyes.

He always told her he loved her hair, too, because it was just like Mama's. She wasn't sure how she felt about having red hair, but Mama told her she'd grow into it.

They sat there on the ground for a few minutes. Then he asked her a question.

"Are you okay with this, Gracie?"

"Then you and Mama really do love Gage and me the same?" She was almost sure sometimes that they loved her baby brother more.

Her father threw back his head and laughed, then stood and pulled her up beside him.

"Let's go home, Gracie Girl.

As they walked away, he held her hand like he did when she was little and they were crossing the street.

Just this once, she let him.

Mercy and Grace

Mercy Beckett and Grace Valentine watched from their rocking chairs. Mercy had told her grandson, Sam, once that she knew for sure they would have rocking chairs in heaven.

As always, she was right.

"That girl is going to be something else, I tell you. Mark my words, Mercy. Mark my words."

Moving to the other side had not stemmed Grace Valentine's bragging when it came to her family. Mercy didn't mind it so much now, though. Besides, she had plenty to brag about herself. She had a great granddaughter who was a fancy doctor up in New York and a grandson who was a Navy SEAL.

"That red hair is something. I bet she's going to be a firecracker." Grace also liked a person with a good head of steam.

Mercy settled back into her chair and pushed gently on the floor of the porch.

The youngsters and their parents had seen some dark times, one way and another. Some she had witnessed firsthand and some from a celestial shore that had a porch and rocking chairs. No doubt, they would see more. That was the way of life. But as the good Lord said, the greatest is love.

And love they had in abundance.

"Grace, let's go get some iced tea."

ACKNOWLEDGMENTS

Thanks to my family who love me even when I am seriously unlovable.

To my Dream Team – Karen Hrdlicka and Joanne Thompson. You make me so much better than I am.

Severe gratitude to Debbie Hoffer and LouAnn Bramante. Being my alpha readers is less about reading and more about being an unpaid psychologist.

To my Beta team – you are the best.

To my Facebook Heifer Squad – as I always say, I don't deserve you, but neither does anyone else, so I'm keeping you.

Thanks to Kim Killion for the gorgeous cover.

A multitude of thank you's to Debra and Drue at Buono Amici Press. They make it all work.

To Freya, Taryn, Maddie, and Tarina – I am so blessed to have you in my life.

Special attention must be paid to Debbie Hoffer. She believed and championed Kyle Valentine when he was just an annoying pain in my ass. We did it, girl. I'll tongue kiss you later.

Finally, to all the readers who support my work – it means more than you can know. You keep reading them and I'll do my best to keep writing them.

Cristin Harber – you know.

Namaste

Anna

ABOUT THE AUTHOR

Anna lives in Tampa, Florida with her kids, grandkids, dogs, various other livestock, and way more books than is strictly healthy. When she is not writing kissing books, she can be found cooking, reading, watching Star Trek, or spending way too much money on Amazon Prime.

Check out my website at *www.annabishopbarker.com*

ALSO BY ANNA BISHOP BARKER

<u>THE FAITHFUL SERIES</u>

Journey To Faithful

Home To Faithful

Faithful Peace

Surviving Faithful

Going Under, A Titan World Novel